Carla Kelly started writing Regency romances because of her interest in the Napoleonic Wars. She enjoys writing about warfare at sea and the ordinary people of the British Isles rather than lords and ladies. In her spare time she reads British crime fiction and history—particularly books about the US Indian Wars. Carla lives in Utah and is a former park ranger and double RITA® Award and Spur Award winner. She has five children and four grandchildren.

Christine Merrill lives on a farm in Wisconsin, USA, with her husband, two sons and too many pets—all of whom would like her to get off the computer so they can check their e-mail. She has worked by turns in theatre costuming and as a librarian. Writing historical romance combines her love of good stories and fancy dress with her ability to stare out of the window and make stuff up.

Janice Preston grew up in Wembley, North London, with a love of reading, writing stories and animals. In the past she has worked as a farmer, a police call-handler and a university administrator. She now lives in the West Midlands with her husband and two cats, and has a part-time job as a weight management counsellor—vainly trying to control her own weight despite her love of chocolate!

REGENCY CHRISTMAS WISHES

Carla Kelly
Christine Merrill
Janice Preston

MILLS & BOON

First published in Great Britain 2017
by Mills & Boon, an imprint of HarperCollins*Publishers*
1 London Bridge Street, London, SE1 9GF

Large Print edition 2018

Regency Christmas Wishes © 2017 Harlequin Books S.A.

ISBN: 978-0-263-07462-8

The publisher acknowledges the copyright holders
of the individual works as follows:

Captain Grey's Christmas Proposal © 2017 by Carla Kelly

Her Christmas Temptation © 2017 by Christine Merrill

Awakening His Sleeping Beauty © 2017 by Janice Preston

This book is produced from independently certified
FSC™ paper to ensure responsible forest management. For
more information visit www.harpercollins.co.uk/green.

Printed and bound in Great Britain
by CPI Group (UK) Ltd, Croydon, CR0 4YY

CONTENTS

CAPTAIN GREY'S CHRISTMAS PROPOSAL

Carla Kelly

To all who believe in the magic of Christmas

Prologue

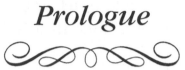

This wasn't a story shared widely. After some thought and a few laughs, New Bedford shipbuilder James Grey and his wife, Theodora, decided to tell their little ones this odd Christmas tale of how they'd met, or re-met, after years apart. They thought it wise to tell it before those same children reached maturity and no longer set much store by St Nicholas. Later, if more adult scepticism took over—well, that was their worry.

It was Christmas story to tell around the fireplace, drinking Papa's wassail and gorging on Mama's pecans nestled in cream and caramelized sugar she called pralines. None of the children's New Bedford friends ate pralines at Christmas, even though many of them had seafaring fathers who travelled the world.

None of their friends had a mother like Mrs Grey, or for that matter, a father like James Grey. If their parents' origins were shrouded in mystery, everyone in New Bedford appreciated the solidity of Russell and Grey Shipworks, whose yards employed many craftsmen at good wages. More quietly whispered about was the boundless charity of Mrs Grey, who assisted slaves to freedom in Canada, or helped free men and women of colour find work in New England.

From the first, a deckhand out of Savannah, to the latest, a young couple fleeing Mississippi and a brutal owner named Tullidge, she and her network of volunteers provided food, lodging, employment and hope.

She was a woman of great beauty, with the soft accent and leisurely sentences heard in the South of the still new United States. James Grey spoke with a curious accent that placed him not quite in Massachusetts, but not quite in England, either. He had a mariner's wind-wrinkled face, and the ships he and his partner built were sound and true. That James adored his lovely wife was obvious to all. That the feeling was mutual was equally evident.

Something about the Christmas season seemed to reinforce this tenacious bond even more. Their oldest friends had heard the pleasant story of how they met in a distant Southern city, after years apart. There always seemed to be more to the story than either party let on, but New Englanders were too polite to ask.

Chapter One

Plymouth, England—October 1st, 1802

'Captain Grey, please excuse what happened. I found this under a box in my officer's storeroom.'

Mrs Fillion held out a letter most tattered and mangled. James Grey set down his soup spoon and picked it up. He squinted to make out some sort of return address. Stoic he may be, but he couldn't help his involuntary intake of breath to see a single word: Winnings.

'What? How?' was all he could manage as he held the delicate envelope as though it were a relic from an Etruscan tomb. Mrs Fillion, owner of The Drake, was kind enough to allow her Plymouth hotel to serve as an informal postal and collection station since the beginning of Napoleon's war. He motioned her to sit down at his solitary table, wishing she didn't appear so upset.

'What happened was that I set a box with some

poor dead officer's personal effects on top of the letter, which I was saving for you,' she said, apologising. 'Unfortunately, I haven't seen you in years.'

'That's because I've operated on the far side of the world for several voyages,' he said. 'Don't let this trouble you.' He stared at the envelope. 'Any idea how long it might have been there?' He found himself almost afraid to open such a fragile document.

He couldn't help wincing when she said, 'It's been there since 1791, because the box I set on top of it had "1792" scribbled on the side.' She sighed. 'Eleven years, Captain. I hope it wasn't something terribly important.'

Likely not. When he never heard from Theodora Winnings after he proposed by way of pen and paper, James Grey, a first lieutenant in 1791, understood a refusal as well as the next man. Since his career seemed to keep him on the far side of the world for much of that decade, he had felt a little foolish for proposing to sweet Teddy Winnings in the first place. Then he dismissed the matter, except when he stood a watch, the perfect time to reflect on so much charm, goodwill and charity in a lovely frame. He stood a lot of watches. Still, Mrs Fillion needed to be jollied.

'I wouldn't worry, Mrs Fillion,' he said. 'I was a brand new first luff and I proposed to a fetching young thing in Charleston, South Carolina. Did it by letter, so you see how callow I was.' He laughed, and thought it sounded genuine.

Mrs Fillion smiled, which relieved him. 'Captain, would you be brave enough to propose in person now, providing the right fetching young thing happens along?'

'Unlikely. I'm a ripe thirty-seven, and serve in a dangerous profession. Why inflict that on a woman?'

'You underrate females, Captain,' Mrs Fillion said.

'I have long been fortune's fool.' He picked up his soup spoon again, giving Mrs Fillion liberty to continue circulating among her other guests.

The dining room was less busy, mainly because of the Treaty of Amiens, which meant most warships were in port, with officers uncomfortable on half pay and scrimping, and crews dumped on shore to starve. War was almost guaranteed to break out again, but until it did, this meant tight times in ports like Plymouth and Portsmouth.

Jem waited until she was engaged in conversation with another officer before picking up the mangled letter. Eleven years was a long time to expect a letter to rule in his favour. Whatever the fervour of the moment, it was long past, whether Teddy's reply had been yea or nay.

He had already finished reading his newspaper, and there was still soup to be downed. Might as well see what she wrote all those years ago. He slit the letter open carefully, dismayed to see water damage inside.

'Yes!' The word leaped out at him. *My God*, Jem thought, *she loved me*. The rest of the letter was mainly blotched and illegible. He stared hard, and fancied he made out the phrases, '…but you need to know…' and then farther down the ruined page, 'I should have…' The box Mrs Fillion set on top of Teddy's letter must have been damp. He could decipher nothing else.

His soup forgotten, Jem leaned back in his chair, staring out the window where autumn rain slid down the panes. His first glimpse of Theodora Winnings was through a fever haze, as though he gazed up at her from the bottom of a pond. That was his second relapse from malaria. Since the frigate *Bold* was peacefully moored in Charleston Harbour, the post surgeon had taken him ashore and left him to the tender mercy of the Sisters of Charity.

He had recalled nothing of the first week except the stink of his sweat and his desire to die. Toward the end of that week, he vaguely remembered a visit from his captain, who announced the *Bold* was sailing to Jamaica, but would return in two months, hoping to find him alive. At the time, he had preferred death. Even in his addled state, Jem knew that was nothing to tell his commander.

By the second week, he could get out of bed for a call of nature, if someone clutched him close around the waist. The Sisters of Charity were tough women who manhandled him so efficiently that any embarrassment quickly vanished.

By the third week, life's appeal returned, especially when Miss Theodora Winnings sat beside his bed to wipe his forehead and read to him. He was still too wasted to pay attention to the words, but he enjoyed the slow molasses sound of Miss Winnings' Southern diction.

By the next week, he spoke in coherent sentences and silently admired the loveliness of her ivory skin, dark hair and eyes and full lips, not to mention a bountiful bosom.

'Captain, your soup must be cold. Would you like more?'

'Oh, no. I'm done.' He looked down at the letter with its nine legible words. 'Mrs Fillion, she said yes eleven years ago.'

He shouldn't have told her, she who set the box on his letter in the first place. He knew Mrs Fillion had been through much, with children of her own at sea, and bad news when her lodgers died in the service of king and country. Her eyes brimmed with tears.

'Look here, ma'am, don't weep on my account,' he added hastily. 'As it turned out, once the *Bold* picked me up and revictualled, we left the Carolinas and never returned. I was a foolish lieutenant. Our paths were destined never to cross again.'

Mrs Fillion wasn't buying it. 'Love doesn't work

like that,' she argued. She dabbed angrily at her tears. 'If you had known her answer, you would have found a way.'

'Poppycock and humbug, Mrs Fillion,' he stated firmly.

He misjudged the redoubtable owner of the Drake. 'Listen to me, Captain Grey,' she demanded.

Unused to being dressed down, he listened.

'I think you should go to the United States,' she said, lowering her voice so the other Navy men couldn't hear. 'Find Miss Winnings.'

'What is the point, madam?' he said, exasperated, more with himself than with her.

'She said aye eleven years ago,' Mrs Fillion replied.

He knew he was wearing his most sceptical expression, but she touched his sleeve, her hand gentle on his arm. 'Have a little faith, Captain.'

He had to laugh. 'Madam, I am as profane a captain as you will find in the fleet, as are most of my associates. We rely on time and tides, not faith.'

'I don't believe you.' She looked around the room. 'I doubt there is a captain or lieutenant in here who doesn't rely on faith, too, say what you will.'

What could he add to that? He wasn't up to a theological argument with a hardworking woman he had long admired. 'I'll think about it,' he muttered, then leaned over and gave Mrs Fillion a whacking great kiss on her cheek. For both their sakes, he chose not to continue the narrative. He could pretend he had reassured her, and she was kind enough to think so, too. That was how polite society worked.

He knew it would be wise to leave the dining room then, and spare Mrs Fillion from more discomfort. He looked in the card room, not surprised to see the perpetual whist game about to get underway. He couldn't remember who had named it that, but during wartime, there was always someone in port to make up a whist table. Some of the officers preferred backgammon, and there was a table for that, too.

Lieutenant Chardon, his parents French *emigrés*, was looking for a partner to sit in the empty chair opposite him. The other two partners, good whist players, were already seated.

'Captain Grey, would you partner me?' the luff asked.

Jem considered their chances of taking sufficient tricks from the proficient pair looking at him with similar calculation. He knew the state of Chardon's purse—his parents dead now, and Auguste Chardon living from hand to mouth, thanks to the Treaty of Amiens. Jem knew they could defeat their opponents, who were post captains like himself, with ample prize money to see them through the irritation of peacetime. Chardon needed a big win to support his habit of eating and sleeping under a roof.

'I'd be delighted,' Jem said, and sat down.

'Our Yankee captain,' one of the opposing captains said, and not with any real friendship.

Jem shrugged it off as he always did. There were worse things to be called. Hadn't his older friend Captain Benjamin Hallowell, also a Massachusetts Yankee, managed to become one of Sir Horatio Nelson's storied Band of Brothers after the Battle of the Nile?

'Aye, sir,' he said, broadening his relatively unnoticeable American accent.

Jem motioned for Lieutenant Chardon to shuffle the deck.Ninety minutes later, he had the satisfaction of watching the captains fork over a substantial sum to Chardon. A note to Mrs Fillion had brought sandwiches and beer to their table. Jem wasn't hungry, but he suspected Chardon was. How nice to see him eat and play at the same time.

After the captains left, grumbling, Chardon tried to divide the money. Jem shook his head. When the lieutenant started to protest, Jem put up his hand.

'I have been where you are now,' he said simply. 'This discussion is over, Lieutenant Chardon.'

And it was; that was the beauty of outranking a lieutenant. He invited Chardon to join him down the street at a fearsome pit of a café serving amazing sausages swaddled in thick bread. He ate one to Chardon's three, bid him goodnight and returned to the Drake, before the lieutenant, not so poor now, could go in anonymity and without embarrassment to his meagre lodgings. In due time if Chardon survived, once war resumed, he would have his own prize money earning further income in Carter and Brustein's counting house.

'You may prefer me not to say this, Captain Grey,' Chardon told him as they parted company. 'You are a man of honour.'

Jem Grey returned the little bow and made his way back to warm and comfortable quarters at the Drake. He could unbutton his trousers, kick off his shoes, lie down on a bed that did not sway with the current, and contemplate his next step, now that he knew Theodora Winnings had loved him eleven years ago.

Chapter Two

After a beastly night worrying how long Teddy Winnings had waited for him to reply to her letter, James scraped away at the whiskers on his face, slouched downstairs to the dining room, and settled for a coffee and a roll, which didn't please Mrs Fillion.

'I really hope you're not still troubled over that unfortunate letter,' she said as she poured him a cup. '*I* worried enough for both of us.'

'No, no,' he lied, then repented because he knew Mrs Fillion was intelligent. 'Aye, I did worry some.'

'What are you going to do about it?'

He looked around the dining room, wishing there were someone seated who had more courage dealing with Mrs Fillion. He saw none, and he knew most of the room's occupants. Men could be such cowards.

'I don't know,' he said frankly.

Honesty appeared to be the best policy with Mrs

Fillion. She declined further comment, to his relief passed on to her next customer, coffee pot in hand.

He had a headful of things to do, but lying awake nearly all night had pushed one agenda directly to the top of his mind's disorderly heap. His jaw ached. A man feeling as low as he did could only take the next step, which he did. He drew his boat cloak tight around him and walked to Stonehouse Naval Hospital.

Unwilling to face the nosy clerks in Admin, Jem walked directly to Building Two, where an orderly met him at the door.

'Where away, captain?' the man asked, in proper navy fashion.

'Surgeon Owen Brackett,' he said. 'Tell him James Grey would like a word, if it's convenient.'

The orderly touched his forehead and gestured to a sitting room. It must not have been convenient for Owen, because Jem sat there for at least thirty minutes. Still in a dark mood, he read through the obituaries in the *Naval Chronicle*, remembering the time he was listed there when his frigate had been declared missing after a typhoon in the Pacific. When the *Nautilus* finally made port in Plymouth a year later, there had been surprised looks from the harbourmaster. He smiled at the memory.

'Jem, what brings you here?' he heard from the doorway.

If Jem had thought he looked tired when he stared

into his shaving mirror this morning, he was a bright ray of sunshine compared to Owen Brackett.

'I thought this damned peace treaty would turn you into a man of leisure,' he said to Owen as they shook hands.

'Hardly. Why is it you deep-water sailors have so many ear infections?' Owen asked.

'Too many watches on deck in storms,' Jem replied promptly. 'If you don't have time…'

'I do. What's the matter?'

Everything, Jem thought. *A proposal of marriage I tendered was accepted eleven years ago but I never saw it.* 'My jaw aches,' he said instead.

Owen gestured for him to come down the hall to his office. 'Have a seat and tip your head back,' the surgeon said. With skilled fingers, he probed, asked a few questions with his hand still in Jem's mouth, and nodded at Jem's strangled replies.

'Tense jaw is all. You've been gritting your teeth for years,' he pronounced. 'It's a common complaint in the navy.'

'Surely not,' Jem said. 'I don't grit my teeth.'

'Probably every time you sail into battle,' Owen countered.

Jem opened his mouth for more denial, then closed it. The surgeon was probably right. 'What's the cure?'

'Peace. Maybe a wife,' Owen replied with a smile. He consulted his timepiece. 'There is a shepherd's pie cooling below deck in the galley. Join me for luncheon? The ale is surprisingly good here.'

They walked downstairs together, the surgeon talking about gonorrhoea with an orderly who stopped him on the stairs with a question. It was more information than Jem wanted or needed, but he couldn't interrupt a friend with no spare time, peace or war. Good thing Owen already had a patient wife.

Owen was right about the shepherd's pie, which had the odd facility of both filling his stomach and loosening his tongue, although that could have been the fault of the ale. A fast eater from years of necessity, he decided to ask Owen's advice about the letter, while the surgeon served himself another helping.

'Here I am, the proud possessor of a letter in which a young woman I love, or at least loved, accepted my proposal,' he concluded. 'I'm curious to know how she has fared through the years.'

'You say she is pretty.'

'Quite, but that's not the half of it. She was so kind to me.'

Even now Jem clearly remembered the loveliness of Teddy Winnings' creamy complexion, and the deep pools of compassion in her eyes at first, followed a few weeks later by lively interest when he was coherent and—he hoped—charming. Young he may have been, but he was a gentleman. He had known he was enjoying the company of a young lady properly raised, and behaved himself.

'Her father ran Winnings Mercantile and Victuallers, a few doors down from the hospital and convent,' he told Owen Brackett. 'It was a substantial business, and I imagine she had plenty of young men interested in her.'

'She's likely long-married,' Owen said.

'Aye.' He hesitated to say more so Owen filled in.

'But you're going to cross the Atlantic and find out, aren't you?' the surgeon asked.

There it was, laid out before him, the very thing Jem wanted to do. Owen knew.

'Better see a tailor right away and get yourself a civilian wardrobe,' Owen said as he stood up and held out his hand.

Jem shook his hand. 'Don't tell anyone. I'm ashore on half pay, but I'm not certain Admiralty House would be happy.'

'Why not?' Owen asked as they headed to the main floor again. 'We're at peace, and that unpleasantness with the colonies is long over.' He took a good look at Jem. 'You want to go back, don't you, and not just for Miss Winnings.' It was a statement, not a question.

'I don't know what I want,' Jem replied frankly. 'I liked living in Massachusetts Colony, but when you're ten years old and your parents pull all the strings...' He shrugged. 'Don't say anything.'

'I'll be as silent as an abbey of Trappist monks,' Owen assured him. 'Bon voyage, friend. Let me know at what longitude your jaw ache ends.'

James took himself to his tailor in the Barbican, who opened his ledger to Jem's previous measurements and congratulated him on maintaining an enviable trimness.

'It's easy enough to do in southern latitudes, when you sweat off every ounce of fat,' Jem said.

Of nightshirts and smallclothes he had an adequate amount. Shoes, too. He assured his tailor that three suits of clothes would suffice, and he could use his navy boat cloak. He reconsidered. As much as he loved the thing, one look would give him away immediately as a member of the Royal Navy, which was perhaps not so wise. He could store his Navy uniforms with Mrs Fillion.

His order complete and promised in two weeks, Jem went next door for a low-crowned beaver hat which struck him as faintly ridiculous, even though the haberdasher assured him he was now *à la mode*. He knew he was going to miss the added intimidation of his tall bicorn, but as Teddy Winnings had told him once—how was it he was starting to remember their conversations?—he was already tall enough.

He paid a cautious visit to the harbourmaster to inquire about any outbound ships headed for the United States. He knew the harbourmaster as a garrulous man. To his surprise, George Headley didn't even blink when he mentioned wanting passage to a former enemy country.

Headley leaned closer. 'This is a special mission, isn't it?' he whispered. 'My lips are sealed, of course.'

'Good of you,' Jem said in the same conspiratorial tone, hoping the Lord Almighty wouldn't smite him dead for deceiving a good, if chatty, man. 'The less said, the better my chances are that none of Boney's spies will hear.'

The harbourmaster nodded, his eyes grave, and gestured toward a fair-sized vessel at anchor in the harbour. 'Captain, the *Marie Elise* is headed to Baltimore, I believe. Would you like me to hail a waterman to take you out there?'

A mere half hour later, he sat in the captain's cabin, drinking Madeira and then forking over passage money.

'We'll sail for Baltimore on or about the middle of October,' Captain Monroe said. 'We're looking at a seven-week passage, give or take.' The Yankee gave Jem a shrewd look. 'You're a seafaring man.'

'I am,' Jem said. 'Royal Navy. It's private business.'

The captain nodded, obviously not believing a word of that, and sounded remarkably like the harbourmaster. 'My lips are sealed. You'll only be a short distance from Washington, D.C. How is it you already sound slightly American?'

'Many people on the Devonshire coast have a similar accent,' Jem hedged, 'but you are right. I was born in the colony of Massachusetts.'

'We two countries need to get along, eh?'

'Indeed we do. I'm lodging at the Drake. Send a boy around when you're ready to lift anchor,' Jem said.

'You've been away a long time from Massachusetts?' Captain Monroe said as he walked topside with a fellow captain, showing him all the courtesies.

'Twenty-seven years,' Jem replied, as he sat in the bosun's chair to be swung over the side to his waiting boat. He wouldn't have minded scrambling down the chains, but he couldn't ignore the American captain's kindness.

'A lot has changed, Captain,' the Yankee said as he motioned for the crew to swing him over now.

I hope not everything. Or everyone, Jem thought as he went over the side and waved to his American counterpart. *Is it too much to hope that Theodora Winnings remains the same?*

Chapter Three

James made a note in his log—personal logs were a habit not easily broken—to let Owen Brackett know when next they saw each other that his jaw stopped aching at Latitude North thirty-eight degrees, four minutes, Longitude West forty-eight degrees, forty-six minutes, roughly the middle of the stormy Atlantic.

The passengers aboard the *Marie Elise* were a disparate lot, some Americans heading home, a French *emigré* or two and Englishmen who were no more forthcoming about their reasons to travel than he was. He had a private chuckle, thinking that some of them might have been what the harbourmaster thought of him, spies or government emissaries.

The crossing was rough enough to keep many of the passengers below deck during the early days of the voyage. Jem had no trouble keeping down his meals, and less trouble standing amidships and looking at oily, swelling water hinting of hurricanes.

He only spent two days in the waist of the ship before Captain Monroe invited him to share the quarterdeck. Jem accepted the offer, scrupulously careful to stay away from Captain Monroe's windward side. From Monroe's demeanour, Jem knew the Yankee appreciated the finer points of quarterdeck manners.

Captain Monroe apologised in advance for some of his passengers. 'Hopefully they'll stay seasick awhile and not pester you with gibes about Englishmen who couldn't fight well enough to hang on to the colonies.' He laughed. 'And here I am, making similar reference!'

'I'll survive,' Jem said, and felt no heartburn over the matter. 'We need to maintain a friendship between our countries.'

'From what you tell me, the United States might be your country, too,' Captain Monroe pointed out. 'D'ye plan to visit Massachusetts during this visit?'

'Perhaps. We'll see.'

Mostly Jem watched the water, enjoying the leisure of letting someone else worry about winds and waves, especially when it proved obvious to him that Captain Monroe knew his ropes. He felt not a little flattered when Lucius—they were on a first-name basis soon—asked his opinion about sails and when to shorten them.

Even better than the jaw ache vanishing was the leisure to recall a much earlier trip in the other direction. He stared at the water, remembering that trip when he was ten years old; he'd been frightened because so-called patriots had torched the family's comfortable Boston house. He remembered his unwillingness even then to leave the colony where he had been born and reared and now faced cruel times.

Looking around to make certain he was unobserved, Jem leaned his elbows on the ship's railing, a major offense that would have sent one of his midshipmen shinnying up and down the mainmast twenty times as punishment. Most painful had been his agonized goodbye to his big yellow dog with the patient, sorrowful eyes and the feathery tail always waving because everyone was a friend. 'I want another dog like you, Mercury,' he said quietly to the Atlantic Ocean.

Papa had named Mercury, because he was the slowest, most good-natured creature in the colony, even after some Sons of Liberty rabble caught him, tarred and feathered him. If Jem's tears could have washed the tar away, Mercury would have survived. He never asked Papa how he put Mercury down, but at least his pet did not suffer beyond an hour or two.

Here he stood, a grown man of some skill and renown among his peers, melancholy over a long-dead dog. As with most complicated emotions that seem to surface after childhood is gone, James wasn't entirely sure who the tears were for.

Contemplating the water through many days of the voyage, Jem found himself amazed at his impulsive decision to bolt to the United States, after reading a mere scrap of a decade-old letter. He knew himself to be a careful man, because he understood the monumental danger of his profession and his overarching desire to see all the officers and seamen in his stewardship as safe as he could make them. Quick decisions came with battle, but this hasty voyage had been a quick decision unrelated to war.

In the cold light of this Atlantic crossing, he justified himself, convinced that the Peace of Amiens, while a fragile treaty, would last long enough for him to make sure all was well with Theodora Winnings and return with Admiralty none the wiser.

Or so he thought. Anything seemed possible, now that his jaw didn't ache all the time and he was sleeping eight hours instead of his usual four. Until this voyage, he had forgotten the pleasure of swinging in a hammock and reading.

As the journey neared its end, he spent a pleasant evening in Lucius Monroe's cabin, drinking a fine Madeira; maybe he drank too much. However it fell out, he told the Yankee skipper about Theodora Winnings and the long-delayed letter.

'Am I a fool for this expedition?' he asked Lucius.

'Probably,' the Yankee replied. 'She helped nurse you back to health from a malaria relapse?'

'Aye, she did. I was a stinking, sweating, puking, pissing, disgusting mess.'

'Then it must be love,' Lucius Monroe joked. 'More?'

Jem held out his glass. 'I never had the courage to ask her why she was even there. There were other women in the ward besides the nuns, but they were all slaves.'

'Who can understand the ladies?' Lucius said. He leaned back and gave a genteel burp that he probably would have apologised for a few weeks earlier, before theirs turned into a first-name acquaintance.

Lucius broke the comfortable silence. 'I've been curious about this since you came aboard, James. You tell me you were born in Massachusetts Colony and spent your first decade in my country. How do you feel about it now?'

'I liked Massachusetts,' he said finally. 'I liked the dock people who didn't mind my chatter, and my friends who took me fishing. My father was next in authority after Benjamin Hallowell, Senior, then serving as Admiralty High Commissioner. Papa let me roam all around the docks.'

He saw by the way the American nodded, that his own childhood had been spent much the same way. 'You understand, Lucius, don't you? There is a freedom here that I cannot explain or understand.'

'Did you come back for another glimpse of that, or of Miss Winnings?' Captain Monroe asked.

'I wish I knew.'

* * *

When the *Marie Elise* docked in Baltimore, James walked down the gangplank, took a deep breath of United States' air, realised it smelled the same as it did in Plymouth, and laughed at himself. With instructions from Captain Monroe, he arranged passage on a coasting vessel to Charleston, South Carolina.

After an evening of good food with Captain Monroe at the curiously named The Horse You Came In On Tavern at Fell's Point, and a night at the inn next door, James boarded the *Annie*, a vessel that deposited him in Charleston a day and a half later, none the worse for wear, even though the vessel was less sound than he liked and the crew even more dubious.

He had stuffed his effects in his old sea bag, which still naturally fit the curve of his shoulder. After a short walk, spent trying to divest himself of the seagoing hip roll, he stood in front of the Magnolia Tavern and Inn, took a deep breath and wondered again what he was doing.

He didn't bother with luncheon. After dropping his duffel in his room that overlooked magnolia trees with their heady blooms, he walked the route from the dock to Winnings Mercantile and Victuallers. At least, he walked to where it should have been, and stared up at a swinging sign that read South Carolina Mercantile. He reminded himself that things change in eleven years, and opened the door.

The smells remained the same—dried cod, pungent tobacco, turpentine. Jem fancied he even recognised the man behind the counter, a fellow with an outmoded wig and a big nose.

'May I help you?' the man behind the counter asked.

Jem relished the soft sound of his speech, wondering how it was that an English-speaking people not so long removed from the British Isles could sound so different. When he was coherent, he had asked Teddy Winnings about that. She had reminded him that African slaves had much influence in the language of the Carolinas.

'Perhaps you can help me, sir,' he asked. 'I came into port here some eleven years ago, when this place was the Winnings establishment. What happened?'

'Mr Winnings died of yellow fever and his widow sold the property to the current owner,' he replied.

That was a fine how-de-doo. Now what?

'Where do the widow and her family live now?' he asked.

The counter man shrugged. 'She didn't have any family. Don't know where she is.'

'No family? I distinctly remember a daughter,' Jem said. Who could ever forget Theodora Winnings and her quiet, understated loveliness? Obviously he hadn't.

'No. No daughter.' A pause. 'Where are you from, sir?'

'Nowhere, I suppose,' Jem said, surprised at himself. 'I am a ship captain.'

'From somewhere north?'

'At one time. No idea where the widow is?'

The shop's front bell tinkled and three men came in. The man at the counter gave Jem a polite nod and dismissed him. 'Sirs, may I assist you?'

Jem took the hint and left the mercantile. He stood a brief moment on the walkway, then turned south, confident the Sisters of Charity hadn't left their convent.

There it was, much the same. He recalled ivy running over the walls, but someone had mentioned a hurricane years ago that had stripped some of it away. The Virgin smiled down at him from her pedestal perch, reminding him of his first view of the statue while lying on his back on a stretcher. With some embarrassment, he remembered shrieking like a girl because she seemed to be falling on him. Oh, those malaria fever dreams.

He rang the bell and waited for quiet footsteps on the parquet floor within. He never prayed much, if at all, but he prayed now that someone would know where Theodora Winnings lived. He squared his shoulders to face the reality that if Mercantile Man said Widow Winnings had no children, then Teddy might be dead, too.

'Don't disappoint me,' he said out loud, not sure if he was trying to exert his non-existent influence on God Almighty, or the world in general, which had been stingy with blessings, of late. He remembered himself and thought, *Please, sir*, that and no more.

Before he could ring the bell again, the door opened on a young face, probably one of the novitiates. In her calm but practical way, Teddy had told him that every yellow fever epidemic meant more young girls in the convent because they had nowhere else to go.

'Sir?' she asked.

He took off his hat. 'I am looking for Theodora Winnings, who used to assist here. Her father owned what is now South Carolina Mercantile. Can you help me?'

She opened the door and he stepped into the familiar coolness that had soothed his fever almost as much as the mere presence of Teddy sitting by his bedside, doing nothing more than holding his hand.

'I will take you to our Abbess, sir,' she said. 'Please follow me.'

He walked beside her down the long hall, breathing in the faint odour of incense and something sharper that still smelled of disease and contagion. Underlying it all was the still-remembered rot of a warm southern climate.

The novice knocked on a carved door, listened with her ear to the panel, then opened it. She stepped inside and motioned for him to wait.

He stood in the hallway during the quiet conversation within, then entered the room when the nun sitting behind the desk gestured to him. The novice glided out quietly.

The nun behind the desk indicated a chair. She clasped her hands on the desk and wasted not a moment on preliminaries.

'I have not thought of Theodora Winnings in years,' the nun said. 'Apparently you have, sir.'

He could blush and deny, but he was long past the blushing stage of his life. 'I have, Sister... Sister...'

'Mother Abbess,' she corrected. 'And you are...'

'Captain James Grey of His Majesty's Royal Navy.'

With that announcement, she gave him a long look, one that came close to measuring the very smallclothes he sat in, down to his stockings. 'I remember you, sir. We despaired of your survival for several weeks.' She permitted herself a smile. 'Even your ship sailed away.'

'With a promise to return,' he reminded her. 'Aye, you have me. I didn't think I would live, either. At times, death sounded almost welcome.'

She chuckled, probably all the emotion her order was capable of permitting. 'Teddy held your hand when we had done all we could.'

It was his turn and he took a page from her no-nonsense book. 'I doubt you knew this, but I left her a letter the morning I walked out of here under my own power to rejoin my frigate. I proposed marriage in that letter, but I never heard from her. I want to know how she is. That's all. The man at the mercantile said Widow Winnings had no children, but that can't be right. Where is she?'

Only an idiot wouldn't have noticed that he had disturbed the serenity of a woman probably committed by oath to be calm in all matters. She stood up quickly and turned her back on him to stare out the window.

'If she's dead, I understand,' he said. 'I want to let her know I would have moved heaven and earth to respond, had I known of her letter's existence. Her letter was misplaced and I only received her reply in September. Granted, eleven years is a long time...'

He let his voice trail away. He knew enough of people to tell, even with her back to him, how upset Mother Abbess was. 'I had good intentions,' he insisted. 'I proposed, after all.'

She turned around. 'You don't understand.'

'Understand what?' he asked, fearful and bracing himself for what, he had no idea. 'Mrs Winnings must have had children. Teddy was one of them.'

'Teddy is a slave.'

Chapter Four

'Shame on her for not telling you,' Mother Abbess said as she sat down.

Astonished, Jem couldn't speak. He took Teddy's battered letter from his inside coat pocket and spread the paltry thing on the nun's desk. He stared at the few legible words through new eyes. 'But you need to know…' suddenly made sense. So did, 'I should have…' farther down the page.

'She didn't come here of her own free will, just to be kind?' he asked, perfectly willing to ignore obvious evidence, even though he understood the shamble of a letter now. *I want to see her anyway*, kept bouncing around in his brain. 'Maybe?'

'No, sir. During fever times, and when we ask, some of the better class of ladies send their slaves here to help.' She made an offhand gesture. 'They're just slaves. If something happens to them…well, you understand.'

'No, I don't,' he said, uncertain if he were more

angry or more appalled at her words. He closed his eyes, which was the only way he could glimpse Theodora Winnings' ivory skin. True, her hair was curly and her lips full, but God above, he had curly hair, too. 'She's so fair-skinned.'

'So was her mother, but by half,' the abbess said. 'Roxie was a house slave and a great beauty. If memory serves me, Roxie was the daughter of a plantation owner and another slave. I assume Mr Winnings fancied her and bought her for his own purposes. Theodora was *their* child, with a quarter African blood, therefore not so noticeably of African descent. It happens all the time.'

Mother Abbess's callous appraisal caused the growing gulf between them to yawn wider by the second. They sat in the same small room, worlds apart. Jem did his best to control the complicated emotions beginning to pinch at his heart like demons from a painting he had seen in a Spanish monastery, thrusting pitchforks into some saint or other.

'I like sailing the oceans,' he said finally. 'The thing I hate the most is patrolling the Middle Passage where we sometimes encounter slave ships.'

He watched her eyes, in his dismay pleased to see some of the complacency in them disappear. 'They stink to high heaven. I have never seen more wretched people, thirsty, starving and chained below decks. Mothers holding their dying babies up to me, as if I could help them. God, it chafed my heart.'

Her face was still serene, but she rattled the beads on the rosary that hung from her waist. 'Why are you telling me this?' Mother Abbess asked.

'I don't know,' he said. 'Should Teddy have said something earlier? I mean before I fell in love with her, because fall in love with her I did.'

'Certainly she should have told you,' the nun said with some vigour. 'More shame to her and good riddance.'

'If you were a slave and you saw a way out of this...this... I don't know what... Would you have said something?' He asked, irritated that his voice was rising.

Silence. The beads rattled louder.

Jem went to the door, eager to leave the suddenly stifling office. 'Can you...or will you...at least tell me where Mrs Winnings took her household, after her husband died and she sold the business?'

Perhaps Mother Abbess saw he was in complete earnest. She joined him at the door to her office. 'Some slaves were sold at auction. Others went with Mrs Winnings to Savannah, where she was from. It was years ago. I doubt any records remain. Leave it alone.'

'I have the time,' he heard himself say. 'I also have the means and the inclination. Good day. Thank you for your ministrations to me eleven years ago. I do owe you for that.'

She opened her mouth to speak, but Jem had no

desire to hear another word. He outdistanced the novice who had seated herself in the hall, and had the satisfaction of slamming the front door hard.

On the other side of it, he shook his head at his own childish behaviour and took a deep breath, which brought a whiff of the harbour, and tar, and the sugary fragrance of gardenias, in bloom in December.

He stood there in front of the convent, angry at himself and wondering if he had wilfully overlooked signs of Teddy's parentage. In Italy and Greece he had seen lovely women with cream-coloured skin like hers. Had he assumed she was of Mediterranean extraction? He looked down at his feet, distressed with himself. Did it even matter? He loved Theodora Winnings.

What now, you idiot? he asked himself, as uncertain as he had ever been in his life. A man across the street was scrubbing steps leading up to a modest house, and children were jumping rope beyond the servant. Jem had the distinct feeling he was being watched so he turned around slowly, and laughed at his folly. It was the statue of the Virgin looking over him.

'Am I an idiot?' he asked her, then felt instantly stupid for talking to a statue.

He felt disgusted with himself for tossing away money and time on a long voyage to the United States, on the highly unrealistic chance that nothing would have changed from the time he sailed away. God Almighty, he had chastised midshipmen at length for that kind of illogical thinking, and now he had committed worse follies than theirs.

His breathing slowed down as he began to admire the pretty statue's carved serenity. He had long harboured the nagging suspicion that his was not destined to be an easy life, or even a lengthy one. A realist, he knew the Treaty of Amiens would only last until First Consul Napoleon felt he was sufficiently prepared with new warships sliding down the ways into the sea around Spanish Gibraltar. The war would begin again in more earnest. When that happened, he did not think it would end anytime soon. Like other men of his class and career, he would have to fight on until the armies wore themselves out, and the seas ran with blood.

The more fool he, that on the Atlantic crossing he had begun to imagine for a tiny moment a happy life with Theodora Winnings, who was waiting for him in Charlestown with love in her heart, even after eleven years. What folly. He had no idea where she was.

He looked at the statue with the modest downcast eyes. 'Any suggestions, madam?' he asked, after looking around to make certain he was still alone on the street. 'Please consider the season. My mother used to tell me that wonderful things happen at Christmas.'

Nothing. *What now, oh, brilliant man?* he asked himself. He could go to Savannah, but for all he knew, Teddy Winnings had been sold down river and wasn't there. He could also travel north to Boston, which he wanted to see again. Admiralty had no idea where he was, and he had enough funds to chase any number of will-o'-the-wisps.

Do I go north or south? he asked himself, uncertain, perplexed, irritated and above all, sad.

As he stood there, he took a deep breath and another. Each breath brought the fragrance of gardenia, roses and other blooms to his nostrils. Cardinals flitted in the trees. He knew Savannah promised more of the same. His chances of locating Teddy Winnings were slim to none, but he could at least spend one warm Christmas, which might render his misery less excruciating. He remembered Christmas in Boston, and decided he had no wish to be cold *and* sad. Warm and sad had more appeal; it also made him smile.

He waited for the idea to sound ridiculous, but it didn't. 'Savannah, it is,' he told the statue, and gave her a little salute. 'What do I have to lose?'

He went back to the shipping office, where the agent behind the counter took his money and informed him that the next coasting vessel would sail on the tide.

'Towers,' he said, and returned some silver to Jem's palm.

'Beg pardon?'

'Towers, *Sir*.'

'I don't understand what you mean by towers,' Jem said, speaking distinctly, and wishing the agent would do the same.

Appearing remarkably put out, the agent pointed to the clock and measured down from two to four.

The mystery was solved. 'Two hours,' Jem said, trying to decide whether to laugh or bang his forehead on the counter. He did neither; a post captain in the Royal Navy has some pride.

He took his ticket and left the office, hearing laughter behind him at his expense. He mentally rehearsed blistering profanity that would make him feel better, but only briefly. He decided in the spirit of the season to be a bigger man than that.

It didn't hurt that the tavern next to the inn had crab cakes, something called okra that luckily tasted better than it looked, and excellent rum. The tavern owner's slave served him well-remembered spoon bread that went down with equal ease. He finished it all with bread pudding and whiskey sauce, staggered back to the inn to pick up his duffel, and took his way to the wharf again, and Savannah.

He knew the distance between the cities wasn't great. He secured a deck chair, propped his booted feet on the railing, and slept.

Chapter Five

A spanking wind off the mainland brought the little coasting vessel to Savannah by midnight. As slapdash as ship's discipline seemed to be, Captain Grey had to give the man at the helm all due honour. Jem knew how tricky it was to sail in the dark near a lee shore, but the captain had managed such a feat, a testament to years of practice from the grizzled look of him.

Jem woke up when he felt a difference in the direction of the wind on his face. He went to the railing and watched as the vessel turned west into the river's mouth and proceeded upstream to the city proper, past the barrier islands of Tybee, Cockspur, Long and Bird, names he remembered from poring over colonial charts when he was much younger. Amazing what a man could remember. Beacon lights burned along the route as the sea diluted itself into the Savannah River.

Now what? he asked himself as the ship docked

right at the wharf, tying up handsomely. Dockside, he looked around, overcame his natural reticence and inquired of a fellow passenger where a man might find an inn.

The traveller gave him a leisurely look—Lord God, didn't anyone do *anything* in a hurry in the South?—and stated his opinion.

'You, Sir, appear to be a man of means,' the man said and pointed. 'Up a street to Bay, turn right and you'll see the Arundel.' He tipped his hat and walked slowly into the night.

Up a street and right Jem went. The Arundel was a two-story affair with the deep verandas he was growing accustomed to. The lobby was deserted at this midnight hour. Opening the door must have set off a bell ringing somewhere, because a man in a nightshirt and robe emerged, rubbing his eyes. In a few minutes, Jem had a room on the second floor. He climbed the stairs, let himself into Number Four and was asleep in minutes.

He slept late, enjoying the quiet, until a soft tap on the door and a quiet 'Sir?' admitted a child with water, towels and soap. Jem took his time washing, shaving and dressing, appreciative of the early morning warmth that signalled life in the South. Dressed and hungry, he opened the glass doors onto the balcony and stood in silent appreciation of the city below.

Coasting vessels and smaller boats carried on the

watery commerce. He wondered how on earth he
was going to find a woman named Theodora Winnings, who was probably married by now and with
some man's name. That is, if she hadn't been sold
downriver to work the cotton, or died years earlier
in one of the regrettable yellow fever epidemics he
knew haunted these shores.

The folly of his enterprise flapped home to roost
on the railing like one of the seagulls he noticed,
squawking with its feathered brethren. He knew
nothing about Savannah. He hadn't a clue what to
do. How did a man find a slave, or anyone for that
matter, in a town where he knew no one? He had
already been the recipient of wary looks because
of his British accent. How would he even know if
anyone would willingly help him? The war for in-
dependence wasn't that long in the past.

He frowned and regarded Bay Street, lined with
shops, some of a maritime variety advertising turpentine, tar and candles. Another sign swung in the
breeze and proclaimed Jephthah Morton to be proficient at tooth pulling.

Jem shuddered and turned his attention to a larger,
better-kept sign next to the tooth extractor, advertising a dining room. He could eat and walk around,
to what purpose he could not have said. Savannah
was too large to go door to door. Had he attempted
that, he could see himself run out of town as a sus-
picious character.

He looked beyond the sign of the bloody tooth and experienced what was probably going to be his only good idea in Savannah. He squinted. The paint was faded, but he could just make out *Savannah Times and Tides*, with *Weekly Broadside* underneath in smaller letters on a building that seemed to lean with age.

He pulled on his suit coat, checked his wallet for money, and walked down the stairs. The fragrance of ham and hot bread coming from the open doors of the dining room was nearly a Siren's call, but he walked past the tooth puller, where someone inside was already screaming, and in the door beyond.

He entered cautiously, because the building seemed to list even more when seen up close. 'Hello? Hello?' he called, and tapped on the doorframe.

No one answered. He sneezed from the veritable army of dust motes that floated in the air, and sneezed again.

The sound brought a man wearing an ink-stained apron out of a closed door. He was as wide as he was tall, with a long beard that looked as though birds of prey had been poking around in it, searching for something edible. Spectacles perched on the end of his nose appeared to hang there in defiance of Newton's carefully thought out law of gravity.

'How may I help you?' Jem heard, and rejoiced that every syllable was enunciated. This was *not* a man from the South.

'You really publish a broadside?' Jem asked. 'I need to place an advertisement.'

The man bowed as far as he could, which wasn't far, considering his bulk. 'Then you will be my first advertiser in a long, long time, sir.' He held out his hand, took it back, wiped off some ink, and held it out again. 'Osgood N. Hollinsworth, publisher, editor and chief correspondent of the *Times and Tides*.'

'Captain James Grey of the Royal Navy,' Jem said as they shook hands.

Osgood N. Hollinsworth blinked his eyes. 'What? Surely we are not at war again and Savannah has already surrendered?'

Not yet, Jem thought. The question made him wonder how long that would be the truth. Already Secretary of State James Madison had warned the Sea Lords in a carefully worded document just what the United States thought about the Royal Navy stopping its ships and confiscating British crewmen.

'No, sir, no war,' Jem said. 'I simply need to place an advertisement.'

'Good thing you came this week, Captain,' Hollinsworth said with a shake of his head. 'I am laying out the final issue. No one in this Godforsaken town reads.'

'Really? It appears to be a prosperous place.'

'Perhaps I am hasty. Commerce here is conducted on the wharf, in the cotton exchange, at the slave auctions and in the taverns, without benefit of newspapers,' Hollinsworth said. 'I am not mistaken when I suspect that these…these…let's call them Southerners…don't trust anyone not from here.'

'Where *are* you from?' Jem asked.

'Somewhere a ways to the west of here. Considerably west,' Mr Hollinsworth said, with a vague gesture.

'I've heard Southerners like to duel at the drop of a hat,' Jem said, half in jest.

Hollinsworth shook a pudgy finger in Jem's face. 'You've never seen happy-triggered men so devoted to honour! Don't run afoul of them!'

'I shan't, sir,' Jem said, still amused. 'About an ad…'

'I can arrange it,' the printer or editor or whatever he was said. 'Soon enough, I will blow the dust of Savannah off my shoes. Do have a seat. I am so overcome by the idea that someone wants to place an ad that I must sit down, too.'

'You mentioned slave auctions,' Jem said, and felt his stomach lurch. Amazing that he could live through years of war and typhoons with nary a flinch in his gut. He knew his sailors referred to him as Iron Belly. Good thing they didn't know how he felt right now, thinking of slaves and high bidders, and Teddy somewhere in between.

'A travesty, those auctions,' Hollinsworth said with a shake of his head. 'Imagine it—a Yankee named Eli Whitney, invented a machine to take the seeds from cotton bolls. Now everyone is rushing to plant more, increasing the need for slaves.' He gave a bleak look. 'But you didn't come here on slave business, did you?'

'No,' Jem lied. 'Years ago, I spent a few months in Charleston, nearly dead of malaria. A young lady nursed me back to health. I hear she lives in Savannah now, and I want to find her.'

That was enough information for a fat little printer with inky hands, Jem decided. Besides, it was mostly true. He had no trouble looking Hollinsworth in the eyes.

What he saw smiling back at him was difficult to comprehend. If he hadn't known better, he would have suspected that this man he had just met saw right through his careful words and into his heart, that organ many a midshipman would have sworn he did not possess. *What in the world?* Jem thought, then dismissed his sudden feeling of vulnerability as the drivel it was. He folded his arms and stared back. 'I will pay you well.'

'Enough for passage to Boston, like you?' Hollinsworth said with a wink.

Do you know something about me? Jem thought, startled again. 'That seems a little high. If you are reasonable, I will be generous.'

Hollinsworth slapped the table between them and the dust rose in clouds. Jem sneezed again. 'Oops! I can be reasonable.'

He named a small sum, which confirmed Jem's suspicions that Osgood N. Hollinsworth was a right jolly fellow, and liked to tease even potential clients. 'That will be fine,' he said, and took the few coins from the change purse in his coat.

A sheet of paper and pencil stub seemed to materialize from thin air while Jem was blinking his eyes from the dust.

'What do you wish me to write?' the publisher said. 'Maybe something like, 'Where are you…insert name? Captain James Grey wants to know. Inquire at the *Times and Tides* on Bay Street.' Insert name?'

'Theodora Winnings,' Jem said and tucked away his handkerchief. 'Could you run it in big letters?'

'I can and will,' Hollinsworth said promptly. 'There isn't much news this week, beyond a warning from the mayor about hogs running loose, and a notice about two escaped slaves.'

'That will do,' Jem said as he rose, eager to leave this dusty shop before he sneezed again. 'Now to breakfast.'

'And I to work,' Hollinsworth said. 'The broadside will be distributed tomorrow. You might wish to walk around Savannah and admire what happens when a town is laid out in an orderly fashion. It's quite unlike your port of Plymouth.'

'How do you know where I…'

Hollinsworth shrugged, and looked at Jem with

that same piercing but kind glance. 'A lucky guess, Captain Grey. The ham, biscuits and gravy next door are superb, and you might discover an affinity for hominy grits. Good day to you.'

Chapter Six

Osgood N. Hollinsworth had been correct about the ham, biscuits and gravy. Nearly in pain from over-indulgence, Jem pushed himself away from the table and paid his bill of fare.

Over the next few days, he realised Hollinsworth had also been right about Savannah, a pretty river town laid out in leafy squares. He came to admire the deep porches and understood their necessity. Summers here were probably blistering hot and drenched with humidity. In the deep shadows of the verandas he saw overhead fans, probably set in motion by the children of slaves doing what they were ordered to do. He couldn't help wondering if Teddy had ever been ordered to fan folks too.

But it was almost Christmas, so the fans remained motionless. He walked, admired the buildings, and breathed deep of magnolia wreaths on many a door of home and business alike. It was far cry from his memories of Boston at Christmas, with wreaths of holly and bayberry, hardy enough to withstand the aching cold. The heady fragrance of magnolia blossoms seemed to reach out to the boardwalk and grab him unaware.

He watched the faces of the city's workers, wondering if he would recognise Teddy Winnings if he saw her. Would she recognise him? A man who stares day after day into a shaving mirror can probably be forgiven if he thinks he has not changed much. For one thing, Jem knew he looked healthier than the pale, shaking malaria-ridden specimen Teddy had tended. He had put on sufficient weight and heft to give himself more of an air of command. Eleven years had done that, too.

His own curly hair was scarcely visible under his hat, mainly because his habits kept it short. He was a man grown, tested and experienced, not a lieutenant just beginning to understand mortality, and think about dangers ahead. Age could do that; so did war.

When the broadside came out the day after he bought his ad, Jem had been suitably impressed with Hollinsworth's effort. The twenty-word plea ran across the bottom of the single page in bold letters impossible to miss. Would anyone read it was the question.

In his anxiety to *find* Teddy without knowing how to do so, he began a little daily commentary to the Almighty, that unknown personage he had been addressing as *Sir* for years. He acknowledged the absurdity of it, but found himself comforted.

Several days passed. In the print shop where no one ever came, Mr Hollinsworth displayed in the window what he insisted was still the last broadside he intended to publish in Savannah. Jem watched for the small stack to diminish as readers put down their pennies, but it remained the same height, to his discomfort. This was no way to find Theodora Winnings, and so he told Mr Hollinsworth, who took his sharp comments in stride.

'I've distributed my broadsides in the squares, too,' the little man said serenely. 'Be patient.'

Jem honestly tried to be patient, going so far as to sit in the back of Christ Church in Johnson Square, the oldest of the squares, according to a shoeshine boy who gave his boots a lick and a promise each day. A choir rehearsed in Christ Church in the evenings, preparing for Christmas services, or so he gathered from their repertory. After supper in the Marlborough Dining Room, he walked the short distance to Johnson Square to listen.

He sat there long enough each night to be greeted eventually by the singers, then asked to join them. He demurred at first, well-acquainted with his own voice. In their polite Southern way, which was beginning to nestle comfortably under his skin, they asked each night until he agreed. By the middle of the second week in Savannah, he attended choir practice three nights a week.

By the end of that week, he also knew his feeble and puny enterprise had failed. How much longer could he stay in this beguiling place remained open to doubt. He had the means to stay for months, but not the inclination. A strange homing instinct was drawing him north toward Massachusetts. He wanted nothing more than to walk those familiar streets and think about his life's direction, something he hadn't questioned in years, but which now loomed large in his agile brain.

He owned to traitorous feelings, if such they were. Why was a respected post captain in the Royal Navy even for the tiniest moment considering a more permanent connection with the United States? He should know better, but he liked it here and America was compelling him to stay. *It's complicated*, he thought, as he listened to Christmas music, walked the streets and squares of a beguiling little city, and wondered about himself as much as he wondered about Teddy Winnings.

The day came when he knew it was pointless to remain any longer in Savannah. He sat on the side of his bed and silently informed *'Sir'* in his now-daily commentary that it was time to move on.

I certainly bear you no ill will, sir, he thought or prayed. He never could decide which it was. *It was a long-odds chance. I know how busy you are at this season, when I suspect many people who pray more than I do want things. I wish it had worked out. Thanks for listening...if you did.*

The day was warm and sunny, much as the day before, and probably as the day after would be. He took his time sauntering to the wharf, breathing in the familiar odour of tarred rope and maritime paint. He waited his turn at the coastal shipping office, aware of his difference among these soft-spoken, slow-moving, congenial folk.

He inquired about a passage north and was informed that he could leave this afternoon on the Charleston coaster, or hang around until the end of the week for a larger vessel being loaded now with cotton and contracted for a Baltimore destination. He decided upon Baltimore. He could take a coach or private conveyance north from there to Boston.

Dissatisfied, unhappy, he walked around that day, stayed awake at night staring at the ceiling.

Tired of his own company and wishing he had cared enough to bathe and shave, he stood on the veranda of the Arundel in the morning, looked toward the print shop and saw her.

Certain he was mistaken, Jem squinted his eyes shut and rubbed the lids. Almost afraid to look, he opened them, and knew the woman across the street, standing there with a broadside in her hand, was Theodora Winnings.

He remained where he was, rooted to the spot, certain she would disappear if he took one step closer. She wore a drab dress, unlike the pretty muslins he remembered. Her hair was invisible under a blue bandanna wrapped around and knotted high on her forehead. He had seen this head covering on slaves in Charleston and Savannah. She was slimmer than he remembered, which told him all he needed to know about her hard life. Holding his breath, he looked down and saw bare feet.

'Good God, Teddy,' he whispered, then addressed his silent partner. '*Sir*, why didn't anyone take care of her?'

It was my job, he told himself. He walked toward the woman he knew he still loved, no matter her circumstances, her race, her current matrimonial status, her anything.

'Theodora,' he said, when he was halfway across the street.

The woman had been staring down at the broadside, and then looking at the dilapidated print shop, as if wondering what she was doing there.

Maybe he was wrong. Maybe it wasn't Teddy. He cleared his throat and spoke louder. 'Theodora Winnings.'

Honest to God, if he didn't feel his heart pound like a drum when she looked at him. He stood still in the middle of the street, barely mindful of a carter cursing at him to move. He gave a don't-bother-me wave of his hand to the driver but consciously willed himself to move.

She stared at him, holding the broadside in front of her as if to shield her body. Slowly she raised it to cover her face, which broke his heart.

He stood right in front of her now. Silently he took the broadside and pulled it away from her face. 'Teddy,' he said. 'Teddy. I owe you such an apology.'

Now that he looked at her, really looked at her honestly, without any of his malaria fever dreams, he could see the smallest trace of Africa. His recent weeks in Savannah had accustomed him to the beautiful shades of dark brown, barely brown, and Teddy's own creamy complexion found on the kindly, patient people who waited on his table, changed his sheets, and ironed his shirts.

'Lieutenant Grey?' she asked, her voice as musical as ever.

He smiled. 'Captain Grey, actually, Miss Winnings, like it says in the broadside,' he told her. 'I grew a little smarter and achieved some rank.'

He wanted her to smile because she looked so serious, with sorrow writ large that he knew was his fault, because he had failed her.

To his dismay, she did not smile. Her shoulders drooped. 'I should have told you,' she said simply, and turned to go.

He reached for her, but she was quicker. 'You don't

want to make a scene here,' she said in a low voice. 'Believe me, you do not.'

He lowered his hand. 'Why did you come then?'

'I had to see you, Captain Grey,' she said and took a deep breath. 'Now I've seen you.'

'But I...' He saw the tears on her face as she kept backing away.

'No,' she said. 'No.'

'*Sir*, this is not fair,' he said out loud. 'Not at all.'

She looked around, as if wondering to whom he spoke, when the door to the print shop banged open and Osgood N. Hollinsworth stood there glowering.

'Get in here right now, Teddy! Your mistress promised me a day's work!'

Chapter Seven

She ran inside the shop as Hollinsworth glowered at her as though she were a disobedient servant. Jem stood in front of the open door, astonished, wondering what power the man had to command someone he probably had never seen. Jem could have staggered under the weight of the whole awful business when he realised that in the eleven years since they had met, Teddy had become subservient and knew when to obey a white man. Either that, or she knew a ruse when she saw one. Jem already knew how intelligent she was.

'*Sir*,' he whispered under his breath to the Lord above. 'Help me know what to do.'

Once Teddy was inside, Hollinsworth's expression changed to his usual cheery demeanour. Jem understood. 'Captain Grey, we're going to let every flying insect into this print shop. Hurry up and come in!'

He hurried, closing the door after him. Teddy stood behind the drafting table, as if afraid of them both.

Her eyes were huge in her face until Hollinsworth bowed from the waist and introduced himself. To Jem's relief, she smiled.

'Miss Winnings, I had to do *something* to get this slow-moving captain out of the street. He doesn't understand Savannah the way we do, does he? Do have a seat, please. No one here is going to harm you.' The printer gestured toward the stool in front of the drafting table. He propped a broom against it. 'If anyone sets the doorbell tinkling, start sweeping.'

Teddy nodded and sat. With a pang, Jem watched her smooth down the rough fabric of the shapeless dress she wore, recognising the graceful gesture from many a time when she sat beside his bed in the hospital in much better clothing. His heart eased, as he realised Teddy was still Teddy.

Jem had to admit that Osgood N. Hollinsworth had a certain charm, something he had not noticed before in their various exchanges. Teddy appeared to relax as the tension left her face. 'Yes, Sir,' she said. 'I can sweep.' Jem saw the dimple in her cheek and relaxed further. 'No one will know I don't belong in here.'

The capable, assured, confident post captain that James Grey knew himself to be had vanished. He stood there like a lump, awkward as though his feet and hands were five times larger than usual. At least so he felt, until Hollinsworth took his arm in a surprisingly gentle grip and motioned him toward the other chair beside the drafting table.

Hollinsworth regarded them with something nearly resembling beatific goodwill toward men. 'Talk,' he said. 'I am going to the Marlborough for some food. Captain, do you have any money? You know what a poverty-stricken editor I am. Why is it writers cannot make an honest dime?'

Wordless, Jem reached inside his coat and took out several bills. 'What do you like to eat, Teddy? I remember macaroons and something with pecans.'

She smiled for the first time, and Jem felt his heart cuddle down into a little pile. 'You remember well… Jem?'

'That's still my name,' he said, even though all he had heard in years was Captain Grey, or something more informal. 'My men call me Iron Belly, but only out of my hearing.'

Her smile grew larger. 'I recall a time when all you did was puke.'

Hollinsworth rolled his eyes. 'My land! Eleven years and this is the best you two can do? I'm going, before I smack you both!'

Jem laughed, and Teddy put her hand over her mouth, a gesture he remembered as though the hospital was mere days ago, when she was a lady and too polite to laugh out loud.

'Fried chicken and greens? Corn bread?' Hollinsworth asked. 'Crab sandwiches?'

'It all sounds wonderful, sir,' Teddy said. 'I haven't had chicken in a long time.'

The door closed, and Jem absorbed the sight of Theodora Winnings, still the loveliest woman he had ever seen, and he had been in many a foreign port since his proposal by letter. He wished he could tell her he had been a chaste, celibate man, but that would have been a lie. He wished he had received her letter years sooner.

He could have said all that; instead, he held out his hand to her. He could have died with delight when she held out her hand and grasped his in a firm hold. Her hands were rough and her grip strong, much like his own. He remembered her delicate touch and the softness of her hands, but much time and many tides had rolled over them both since he wrote that letter and she answered it.

She opened her mouth to speak. He held up his free hand, ready to break a social rule.

'A gentleman would let you speak first, Teddy, but I have to start. I won't have you apologise for anything when I owe *you* the apology.'

It didn't work. 'Jem, I'm a slave. I always was. I never told you.' Her voice was low and earnest. 'It was wrong and I've regretted it for years. May I please apologise first?'

'No, you may not.' He felt like he floundered, but he was still a man used to command. 'Teddy, I didn't get your letter until September.' He reached in his pocket and pulled out the fragile thing, setting it carefully on the drafting table. 'You see what I could read. Mrs Fillion had set a box on top of it, and there it remained for years.'

'You told me to send a letter care of the Drake,' she said. 'Her hotel?'

'We officers of the fleet based in Plymouth have long used the Drake as an informal place to store our personal effects. Everyone passes through there sooner or later,' he explained. 'What happened in this case is that the owner of the box on top of your letter died.'

'So there it sat,' she said with a sigh.

'Every so often, Mrs Fillion advertises in the newspaper, listing the names and property, hoping next of kin will claim the items,' he said. 'Someone finally did. I happened to be in port when she found the letter underneath.'

'And you dropped everything and ran away to the United States? Captain Grey, I don't remember you as an impulsive person. Aren't you at war? Did you bring your frigate with you?'

The way her eyes twinkled made him laugh. Funny how they had picked up where they left off. When his malaria fevers had begun to subside and he lay there in the convent, stupefied and even unsure where he was, Theodora Winnings had jollied him out of the doldrums by reading a book of wise remarks and tomfoolery by Benjamin Franklin. He knew she liked to laugh, and by God, he could have used a few laughs in the past decade.

'There *is* no war right now. First Consul Bonaparte has foisted the Peace of Amiens on us.'

'That's a good thing, I would imagine, Jem.'

He smiled to hear her affectionate name for him. Amazing how eleven years could nearly vanish. With a start, he realised that since his parents' deaths years ago, no one called him that except Teddy Winnings.

'Amiens is good for me,' he assured her. 'Most of us post captains were thrown ashore on half pay, which meant I could book passage on the first ship to the United States and the Royal Navy is none the wiser.'

'You came all this way without knowing even where I was or whether I was alive or dead?' she asked.

He heard the wonder in her voice. He could assure her that was the truth, or he could be honest. Which would it be? He knew now she was a slave, a woman of Ashanti or Ibo origin two or three generations back, someone who had to bend to the will of others. He could chat with her, satisfy himself she was well, and leave for Baltimore at the end of the week, as planned.

He might have done precisely that, if he had not looked into her eyes and remembered what it was beyond her amiability and breathtaking beauty that made Theodora Winnings so memorable. Kind eyes looked into his and he recalled with delight her amazing ability to give whomever she was talking to her complete and undivided attention. He knew it was a rare gift. He would be honest, because she was paying attention to him, completely focused.

'Teddy, I wanted to assure myself that you were alive,' he said. 'I had no doubt you would be married and with a family of your own.'

'Not this slave,' she said. 'Why else are you here then?'

He couldn't help looking around to make sure British spies weren't pressed against the front window, peering in and listening. *I'm an idiot*, he thought, suddenly weary.

'You can tell me,' she said, putting her hand over his. 'I don't expect you to come to my rescue. You had no idea I even needed rescuing. What else?'

Her hand was warm. He turned his over and interlocked their fingers. 'Teddy, I wanted to go home again to Massachusetts. After I assured myself that all was well here, I was…well, I am…taking ship north to Baltimore and then to Boston.'

He felt her fingers tremble and tightened his grip. 'You told me eleven years ago how a howling mob burned your house when you were a boy, killed your dog, and sent you all fleeing north to Halifax,' she said. 'Why would you ever want to return there?'

'I liked Massachusetts,' he said simply. 'I wish I

had a better explanation. Have you ever just *liked* something?'

She nodded. 'Since we are truth telling and it sounds to me like you've already booked passage...' Her voice trailed off and he heard the regret. It might have been wistfulness, or even envy that he could travel about on a whim.

'Have you?' he asked.

'I liked *you*,' she said, her brown eyes claiming his total attention. 'You sailed away at Christmas, Jem. Every year I wondered how you were doing. I lit a candle every year at Congregation de St Jean-Baptiste, hoping you were still alive.' She broke off her glance. 'I wasn't going to this year. I was done with it.' She looked up and he felt his heart start to beat again. 'But here you are, at least for now. I know you are alive and I suppose that must suffice.'

'Then why are you crying?' he asked, his voice soft.

Chapter Eight

The shadow of a man passed the door and Teddy gasped, tears forgotten. She grabbed the broom and began to sweep a floor that looked as though it had not been touched in a generation. Dust flew and Jem sneezed.

When the footsteps receded, Jem grabbed the broom. 'Hey now, lady, he walked on by.'

He tried to pry the broom from her grasp, but Teddy was strong and hung onto it. 'You don't understand that I am a slave and this is the South,' she said and yanked on the broom. 'Let go.'

Jem released the broom, acutely aware of the terror in her eyes. He watched her edge toward the door and knew he had no incentive to keep her there, if she wanted to leave. Her fear told him chapter and verse of what could happen to a slave alone with a white man. Eleven years had changed Theodora Winnings even more than it had changed him. Better keep talking.

'When I did not hear from you, I was moderately philosophical about the matter, I'll admit,' he told her. 'Who was I, after all? A Royal Navy first lieutenant barely alive and still shaky. I assumed you were the pampered daughter of a Charleston merchant, determined to do good in a fever hospital. I was nothing but very small fry.'

As practical as he remembered, Teddy shook her head. To his relief, she put down the broom and moved away from the door, not far, but far enough to give him reason to hope. It began to matter to him more with each passing minute that she not leave.

'Captain Grey, no one volunteers at a fever hospital,' she said, enunciating each word in a most un-Southern way. 'Mr Winnings hated it, but Mrs Winnings volunteered me all the time. I had no choice.'

'My God, what kind of woman is she?' he asked.

'A sad woman who could not produce any children of her own and could only look on as I was born and cherished by her husband,' Teddy told him. 'He even taught me to read and write, which is illegal, I assure you.'

'White folks are afraid you'll get ideas?' he asked, unable to mask his disgust.

'Most likely.' She sat down. She smiled at him, and years fell away. 'Don't get a swelled head, Captain Grey, but going to the fever hospital became the best part of my week.'

The smile left her face soon enough and she settled into that neutral expression he had seen on many a slave's face in his brief tenure in the South. 'I should never have walked through the convent grounds with you when you started feeling better.'

'Probably didn't have a choice, did you?' he asked, his understanding growing of Theodora Winnings' life spent balancing on the tightrope of keeping Mr Winnings happy and not irritating Mrs Winnings too much.

'I did, actually,' she said. 'For all that they were cloistered, religious women and unacquainted with actual life, some of the nuns could see what was happening between us. They told me I should find another patient, or at least tell you of my parentage.' Her expression softened. 'They didn't order me away, however.'

As he watched her, Jem wondered how easy it would have been to ignore that ruin of a letter Mrs Fillion gave him. He could still be in England, restless at being ashore on half pay, and thinking about nothing more interesting than what he would be having for dinner that night. All things considered, this was better. Come to think of it, any time at all in Theodora Winnings' gentle orbit was better. Maybe this was his odd little Christmas gift from St Nicholas.

She sat back on the chair, her guard down again. 'Every morning before I went to the hospital, I told myself it would be the last time. I ordered myself to tell you I was a slave, and every morning, I could not.'

In for a penny, in for a pound, he thought. 'The thing is, Teddy, it would have changed nothing,' he said and took his own deep breath. 'I remain firm in my resolve.'

'You can't be serious,' she replied.

'Never more so.'

'Even if you know any sort of…connection between us is impossible?' she asked.

He shrugged. 'Why? I assume you could not tell me the truth because you loved me.' He touched the ruined letter on the drafting table. 'Your letter confirmed it eleven years ago.'

Teddy opened her mouth to speak, then gasped as another shadow approached the door and opened it. She leaped to her feet and crouched behind the drafting table as Osgood Hollinsworth opened the door, bearing a pasteboard box of food.

Go away and let me talk to this lady, he wanted to shout as Mr Hollinsworth set the box on the desk.

'You can talk after we eat,' the printer said. 'I'm not going anywhere until we do. Chicken, greens, Johnny cake!'

How was it that this round little man seemed to know what he was thinking? *I am losing my mind*, Jem thought, exasperated.

'Captain Grey! Coax that pretty miss out from behind my drafting table. You can be as high-minded as you wish, but we need to eat. You know, as we puzzle out what to do.'

'There is nothing we can do,' Teddy Winnings said as she left her hiding place and sat where Mr Hollinsworth pointed.

Hollinsworth blinked his eyes in surprise and clucked his tongue. 'Missy, you have a lot to learn. Doesn't she, James?'

Hollinsworth looked from one to the other, smiling as though all was well in the world. 'Must I do all the thinking?' he asked the air in general. 'Eat something.'

Maybe the chance was gone. Teddy seemed almost relieved not to venture deeper into their conversation. She arranged the food, setting it just so, as if seeking order to a life suddenly out of kilter.

So be it. He was hungry. He could be superficial, too, although for how long he did not know. The chicken was tasty enough for Jem to ask her, 'Miss Winnings, can you cook like this?'

'Certainly, sir,' she said, after she chewed and swallowed. 'I can cook chicken anywhere.'

'Don't be so…so…blamed trivial!' Hollinsworth declared, and waved a chicken leg for emphasis. 'Miss Winnings, how did you find my broadside? Just curious.'

The soul of manners, she wiped her fingers delicately on a piece of newsprint. 'It was the strangest thing, sir. I was hanging up the wash today when the broadside just sailed into the yard on that high wind, and dropped in my hands.'

'There wasn't any wind this morning,' Jem said, reaching for another chicken piece.

'There was,' she insisted. 'Are you a wind expert?'

'Actually, I am. No wind,' he said firmly.

She gave him a look that would have skewered a lesser man. 'Wind. The broadside seemed to attach itself to my hand. Don't laugh! I dropped everything and came here. You don't know everything, Captain Grey.'

I like this spirited Theodora, he thought, but decided wisely to keep his comments to himself. 'I bow to your greater knowledge,' he said, unable to resist some repartee, even as he longed to yank the conversation back to her words spoken just before the printer opened the door.

Hollinsworth, damn the man, seemed to have other ideas. 'Miss Winnings, enlighten us. What happened after your father's death?'

She glanced at Jem, apology in her eyes, but obedient in her attention to the printer. Jem decided that the intervening years must have been a harsh school for a slave who lost her only advocate with her father's passing.

'Mrs Winnings sold the business, bought a house and moved us here.' She shook her head over a thigh fried a crispy brown. 'Savannah was her childhood home.'

Jem took heart when she turned to him and touched his arm. 'Jem, Mr Winnings died not long after that Christmas when you sailed away. He died in January of ninety-one. When I was tending him at home because he could no longer go to the mercantile, Mr Winnings showed me his will, already notarized. Upon his death, I was to be freed and provided with two hundred dollars.'

Sudden tears spilled onto her cheeks. 'Jem, when the will was read, there was no mention of my freedom or any money. When I asked Mrs Winnings about it in private, she said solicitors could be easily unconvinced.' She put her hands over her ears. 'I can hear her still.'

In the silence that followed, Jem could almost hear Mrs Winnings, too. He thought of his own life in those few months since he had left Teddy the letter, hopeful she would answer, determined to return for her, despite duty and war. Time passed. He never grew any more in stature—he was tall enough—but he grew in cynicism and then a complacent sort of acceptance, where Teddy was concerned.

'I wish I had known,' he said. 'If only there was a way to know instantly what goes on in others' lives.' It was absurd, but he had to say it.

Teddy gave him a faint smile. 'You can't imagine how I prayed you would find out and save me. I prayed and prayed. Nothing.'

He bowed his head in sadness at the same time Mr Hollinsworth blew into his handkerchief, muttering something about being stretched too thin, which made no sense to Jem. At least the man felt like crying in solidarity with them. How could he be busy? Nothing seemed to happen in Savannah.

'She sold the business and moved here,' Jem said. He put down the chicken thigh, hungry no longer.

Teddy nodded. 'She bought a house near Ellis Square. It burned in the fire of ninety-six and we moved to a smaller house on the edge of Green Square.'

How many times have I walked by it in the past two weeks? Jem asked himself. He amended his thought. He had only walked there once, because it was a ramshackle area, unsafe. 'I've been here long enough to know that as a come down,' he said.

'It was,' Teddy replied. 'She started selling off her slaves.' He heard the sob in her throat. 'My friends!'

He stared into her eyes, chagrined to see that deep gaze of men who had been in combat on sea and shore. He knew he had that same stare, but he had never seen it in a woman's eyes before and it unnerved him.

'Theodora...'

'I am last,' she said quietly. 'I believe I was her hedge against ruin.'

Chapter Nine

Reticence be damned. Jem took her arm, pulled her toward him and held her while she sobbed. Between breaths that shook her, she murmured something about card games and one losing streak after another. He listened in horror and heard the dreary pattern of a desperate widow gambling at cards, trying to recoup some shred of a formerly prosperous life.

He glanced at Mr Hollinsworth, who seemed involved in sorrow of a different sort, an inward examination. Jem had not known the man a few hours before he had seen him as a jovial fellow, with ready quips. Who was this new fellow?

He held Teddy close on his lap and realised he had not been a callow fool in 1791, infatuated by a pretty face and figure. He had told his story a few times in frigate wardrooms, usually to hoots of laughter, until he had begun to think perhaps he had been a naive boy, recovering from illness, who mistook kindness for attachment of a more permanent nature.

He held her, felt her tears dampening his coat, and understood the nature of what he had felt in 1791, love so deep it shook him even now. 'Help me, *Sir,*' he whispered to that friend of his.

He glanced at Mr Hollinsworth just then to see him nod ever so slightly, his own countenance anything but trivial, or jovial, or shallow or any of those weary adjectives describing someone lightweight.

'Aye, laddie,' Mr Hollinsworth said.

He let Teddy's tears run their course, pressing his handkerchief into her palm. 'Blow your nose and dry your eyes,' he said. 'I will return with you to Green Square and I will buy you. I didn't come here penniless.'

She didn't bother with his instruction, beyond wiping her nose, her face stained with tears. 'You're too late. She sold me yesterday to William Tullidge. I am only hers until after Christmas. She insisted.'

Mr Hollinsworth gasped. 'He's one of the richest men in Savannah. Cotton, land, slaves.' He shook his head. 'Influence.'

'Then I will buy you from him,' Jem said, undeterred. 'What did he pay?'

'Two thousand dollars,' she said, then looked away, unable to meet what he knew was his own horrified gaze. 'Do you have that much money?'

He shook his head. He had more, clearly outlined

in a legal letter of transfer from Carter and Brustein to any counting house in North America, but such a transfer took months. 'Not on hand.'

'Then I am ruined,' Teddy said. Dignified even in her despair, she got off his lap, straightened her dress and started for the door. She turned back to give him the level gaze that told him he commanded her total attention.

'Captain Grey, I came here for one reason only. I know there is nothing you can do to save me, at this point.'

'But I can tr—'

She help up her hand. 'Stop. Let me speak. I came here solely to see you. I came here to assure my eyes—no my heart—that you are well and whole now. I came here to apologise...' She gave him a fierce look that closed his mouth again. 'Deny that you came here for the same reasons only. I dare you.'

She had him. 'I came here for those precise reasons,' he admitted, because it was true.

Her hand was on the doorknob now. He knew he had lost, but he had to try once more. He knew what he had to say would brand him forever in her eyes as a fool, but he had to try. He glanced at Mr Hollinsworth for... For what, he had no idea. Support? Compassion? Empathy? And he saw an amazing sight.

Somehow, the little round man seemed to grow a foot taller. His eyes bored into Jem's eyes, telling him without words that he had a potent ally in this odd quest that had turned into a mission so important that he felt it in his entire being.

'Listen to him, Theodora,' Mr Hollinsworth said, and it was no suggestion.

'Something happened in Charleston,' Jem began.

Maybe Teddy felt something unusual in the dusty room, same as Jem did. Whatever it was, she walked back and sat on the stool.

'I learned who you were in Charleston, and it didn't send me rushing to take ship back to England,' he said. 'I stood outside the convent and I must have prayed. Me! I never pray.'

He looked for scepticism in those lovely eyes and saw something else. Eyes still cast modestly toward her bare feet, she smiled.

He couldn't help his sudden intake of breath. 'Teddy, that statue,' he said, and couldn't think of words, he who had commanded, and fought, and blistered his frigate's air with admonition.

Total silence filled the room. He watched dust motes dance. Theodora didn't raise her gaze. She placed her hand near her heart. He waited, barely breathing.

'You sailed in December of 1790,' she said. He leaned forward to hear her soft words. 'In September of ninety-one, a hurricane struck the city.' Her breath came quicker. 'The statue outside the convent literally blew away. The winds stripped all the ivy from the buildings. Such a storm.'

As she raised her eyes to his, Jem remembered to breathe. 'My father commissioned another statue, one in stone this time. I was the model. It was the last thing he did before he died.' She hesitated.

Now what, he thought. *Now what?*

'I think you should challenge William Tullidge to a duel,' Mr Hollinsworth said, and rubbed his hands with something close to glee.

'He'll shoot me dead,' Jem said immediately. 'I am a terrible shot.'

The room grew silent again, as the others seemed to expect Jem to say more. 'A duel is nonsense. I can offer the man a down payment and see if he will wait three or four months for my money to arrive.'

'Tullidge is impatient and used to matters falling out in his favour,' Mr Hollinsworth said. 'I doubt he ever waited a week for a dime owed him.'

'We have until the day after Christmas,' Teddy said, dignified as he remembered, but with something else. He could nearly feel her excitement, as though the wheel was suddenly turning in her direction.

'What about Mrs Winnings?' Jem asked. He felt sweat dripping down his back as he contemplated staring down the muzzle of a pistol aimed at him. 'Could she stave him off? What was the nature of this devil's bargain the two of them made?'

'Mrs Winnings has finally lost all the money she received for Papa's store. Her house burned in the fire six years ago,' Teddy told them both. 'She gambles at cards...'

'Badly, I would say,' Mr Hollinsworth said.

Teddy sighed. 'She is always certain the next turn of the card will recoup her fortune. I fear gamblers are like that. She staked her house, a poor ruin of a place, mind you, on the turn of the card and lost it.'

'He played her deliberately, didn't he?' Jem asked.

'Emphatically yes,' she replied. 'He's been eyeing me this past year and more, and it unnerves me. He promised she could keep her house and he would give her two thousand dollars for me.' She paled visibly at her own words and covered her face with her hands. 'She was saving me for an emergency, Jem.'

'That is an unheard-of sum,' Mr Hollinsworth said, his face pale.

It's not a penny too high for someone as beautiful as Theodora Winnings, Jem thought, shocked, too, but not as surprised as the printer.

'I was her insurance against total ruin,' Teddy said, and bowed her head.

That was all she needed to say. Jem thought about the barrel of that pistol, then dismissed it. He had been on lee shores before, when nothing good was going to happen unless he and his crew exerted supreme effort. His crew had never failed him. He looked around at his crew—Teddy, and a fat printer from somewhere—and grinned at them.

'Teddy my dear, I can't explain this, but when I looked at your statue in Charleston I felt some odd assurance that things would work out in my... in our favour. I didn't even know where you were, but something told me to go to Savannah. I know it's nonsense, but what is that, measured against a duel to the death with a Southern gentleman?'

His crew laughed, indicating they were as certifiable as he was. Emboldened by their reaction and amazed by his own words, James Grey, usually a thoughtful man who never performed a hasty act, remembered Mrs Fillion's admonition in Plymouth and decided to have faith.

Further emboldened, he kissed Theodora Winnings' cheek and told her to go home before she got into trouble with the silly gambler who had controlled a good woman far too long.

'Heaven knows you are probably in trouble with Mrs Winnings right now,' he said, as he opened the door for her. 'What will she do?'

'She has a silver-backed hairbrush,' Teddy said with touching dignity. 'It hurts.'

He stared at her in shocked silence, realising how naïve he was.

'Too bad I cannot duel with her, too,' he said, pleased with himself that he controlled the anger threatening him. 'Do you dare leave her house in the evening?'

'She goes to her room by nine of the clock,' Teddy said.

'I'll be at Christ Church then.' He couldn't help a chuckle, even as he wondered why in God's name he had any right to be cheerful, not with death by duel on his menu this week. No doubt about it: In the past few months, he had gone through more emotions than Edmund Keene on the Drury Lane stage. 'The choir has asked me to join them in Christmas carols.'

'I didn't know you sang,' she said.

'I didn't either, Teddy,' he told her, and kissed her lips this time, something he had wanted to do for the past eleven years. 'There's a lot I didn't know, before I ran away to the United States.'

She smiled at that, touched his cheek for a too brief moment with the palm of her hand, and left the printing shop. He watched her hurry away, looking right and left, maybe hoping no one had seen her. Usually a bustling, busy thoroughfare, Bay Street was surprisingly empty. He chalked it up to an unexpected blessing.

'Well, now, Mr Osgood N. Hollinsworth,' he began, turning back to face the printer, 'since you seem confidently sanguine that I should challenge a poor specimen of manhood to a duel, do you have any idea how I can survive it and live happily ever after with the woman I love?'

'Not one single idea,' Hollinsworth assured him cheerfully. 'I have found in life that it's often best to make up things as I go along.'

'I wish I found that reassuring,' Jem replied. 'Where away?'

'The residence of Mr William Tullidge, Esquire,' Hollinsworth replied. 'You have a date with destiny.'

'I wish you wouldn't look so cheerful,' Jem groused.

'Have faith, Captain. Didn't you just say that?'

'I did,' Jem replied, his mind resolved. 'Lead on, sir. What could possibly go wrong?'

Chapter Ten

To call William Tullidge's residence in Ellis Square a mansion without equal would be to denigrate it. Even in his occasional hurried visits to London, Jem had never seen a house so well suited to its surroundings and beggaring any description except magnificent. He stared in open-mouthed wonder, his terror at the approaching encounter momentarily forgotten.

'Pardon me, Mr Hollinsworth, but what pays this well in Savannah, a town that we will agree is pleasant, but not a metropolis?'

'Slavery, Captain, pure and simple,' his companion said. 'He has built an empire with a lash on the backs of souls bought with blood money. He raises some cotton, but deals more in slaves.'

Startled by the intensity in the generally congenial voice of the printer, Jem stared at Hollinsworth. 'Sir, with your vehement views, I am astounded you didn't shake the dust of the South off your shoes years ago.'

'I had my reasons for staying, Captain,' he replied, and there was no mistaking the grim cast to his countenance. 'I have almost satisfied them and will leave soon.'

'He's not going to see things our way, is he?' Jem asked calmly enough, considering how his heart started to bang against his ribs.

'Unlikely,' Hollinsworth said, but he seemed to have inexplicably regained his good humour. 'I should warn you that he bears no love for the Royal Navy that burned his plantation on Tybee Island, among others, during our late unpleasantness.'

Jem took a good, long look at Mr Osgood N. Hollinsworth. 'Why do I have the nagging suspicion that you are *enjoying* this whole business?'

Trust the old rip to drag out a flippant response. 'Captain, at times it seems as though centuries pass in my life where nothing much happens. Oh, there is always the usual, but you and Miss Theodora Winnings have piqued my interest.'

'I am not reassured,' Jem said dryly. 'Ah, well. I'm in too deep to back out.'

'I hoped you would say that.'

Jem gave him a withering look and walked up the steps to the imposing front doors. He noticed the pineapple carved into the woodwork over the door.

'I remember this from Massachusetts,' he told the

fat man puffing along behind him. 'Hospitality's symbol?'

'I wouldn't hold my breath, Captain,' Hollinsworth said, as Jem knocked on the door.

A butler ushered them in and suggested they wait in the hall, once Jem stated he was Captain James Grey, Royal Navy.

'If what you say is true, that should at least get the man's attention,' Jem said. 'My mere mention of the Royal Navy kept us out of the sitting room, eh?'

It did. Jem stood in a foyer of stunning beauty, with a parquet floor of some intricacy and what looked like leather wall coverings with an embossed design. *Built on the backs of slaves, eh?* Jem thought, as he admired and deplored at the same time.

'Here he is,' Hollinsworth said under his breath, as a man older than Jem came down the central staircase, looking not a bit pleased.

'What business can I possibly have with the Royal Navy?' he asked with no preamble, no bow and certainly no hand extended, either.

'Theodora Winnings,' Jem said, determined to be as brief as the man with rancour in his eyes who stood before him. 'Mr Tullidge, I am Captain Grey, and I wish to acquaint you with my interest in that lady.'

'Lady? You've been misinformed.'

'Lady,' Jem repeated firmly. 'I met her years ago in Charleston and proposed matrimony by way of a letter. Her reply in the affirmative went astray for eleven years. I am here now, and I intend to claim her.'

'You intend to claim her?' Tullidge asked. He laughed. 'You intend to *claim* her? I won her in a game of piquet. Mrs Winnings belies her name. She *never* wins, and we all know it.'

How distasteful, Jem thought. 'Apparently you and friends of yours play cards with her, knowing you will win.'

'We do. Should be ashamed of ourselves, shouldn't we?' he asked, unrepentant.

James saw no point in dignifying such meanness with a comment. He remained silent.

'Poor, poor Mrs Winnings never could figure out what to discard.' Tullidge shrugged. 'A little loss here, a little loss there. She finally gambled away her house, and then she gambled away her last slave.' He made a sad face at Jem that was utterly overruled by the triumph in his eyes. 'Poor, poor you.'

'I love her,' Jem said. It was the first time he had said the words out loud, and they felt so good. 'Do you?'

'Love? She's a slave and I fancy her.' Tullidge laughed again. 'Too bad your letter went astray, Captain. It fairly breaks my heart.'

'Miss Winnings told me you have guaranteed her mistress her house again, plus two thousand dollars,' Jem said. He felt like the last cricket of summer, chirping on a hearth, with winter coming. 'I will offer you five hundred dollars now against another two thousand, once my letter of credit and remittance is approved in a Savannah counting house of your choice.'

'How long will that take?' Tullidge asked. 'Three months? Four months? Longer?'

'It will come,' Jem said.

He knew disappointment was the only outcome of this conversation. He knew that before he knocked on the door, but a man has to try. 'Does she mean anything to you?'

'Certainly not,' Tullidge said, 'but Lord, she is a beauty, even if she is too old for my tastes, really. A year or two and I will sell her.'

Jem heard a great roaring in his ears and felt an ache in his jaw unlike anything he had experienced before. This was worse than combat, worse than bringing his frigate alongside the enemy and pounding away at close range. The tender woman he loved was at stake. He felt a great helplessness, he who was renowned in both fleets for his capability under fire and his innate sense of what to do when there was nothing to do.

'I want to buy her, free her, and marry her in a northern state,' he said, pressing on doggedly because he had to, even when there was no hope. 'My intentions are honourable.'

'You are a member of a hated nation to me, Captain Grey,' Tullidge declared. 'You damned British burned my plantation on Tybee Island and scattered my slaves and I could do nothing. Nothing!'

His voice rose to great heights. Out of the corner of his eye, Jem saw heads pop out of doors, and withdraw just as quickly.

I'm not even British, Jem thought, taking a tiny moment to marvel that in the space of one awful interview, he had admitted two things to himself—he loved a lady and he wasn't an Englishman. Amazing how a fraught situation had sharpened his senses.

'I take it your answer is no?' he asked calmly, and smiled because it sounded humorous to him. Might as well go down with the ship. Standing there in the foyer of a mansion built with blood and belonging to one of Savannah's most influential citizens, Jem felt strangely calm.

Tullidge laughed at him, and Jem joined in, which made the slaver stop and stare. 'By God, you're a cheeky fellow.'

'And you, sir, are a bona fide, certified, dyed-in-the-wool bastard,' Jem said, crossing a barrier and committing himself to death. 'I challenge you to a duel.'

Tullidge stared at him, his expression incredulous. He turned around and shook his head at nothing, then whirled around so fast his coattails flared out.

'Why not? I doubt you are much of a shot, and

it will be duelling pistols. You challenged so the weapon is my choice. When do you plan to be shot?'

'Tomorrow at eight in the morning. I don't want to waste my time in Savannah,' Jem replied. 'A freighter jobbing to Baltimore will pass down the channel around that time, and I don't want to miss it.'

Tullidge's eyes widened in surprise, but he did not laugh. The colour left his face. 'Eight of the clock at my *burnt-out mansion!*' He shouted the words but Jem did not flinch.

'Do you have a second?' Tullidge demanded. 'A surgeon? Do you even have a clue what the rules are in Code Duello?'

'Not one,' Jem said, getting into the mood of this. 'I'm a dreadful shot.' He turned to Osgood Hollinsworth. 'Will you second me?'

'Absolutely,' the printer said. 'Wouldn't miss it. I even know a good surgeon. What say you two go back to back, march fifteen steps, turn and fire?'

'Sounds fine,' Jem said. 'Tomorrow morning then, Mr Tullidge? If you change your mind, I'm staying at the Arundel. Good day, sir. Looks a bit like rain.'

Jem turned on his heel and marched out of the foyer, Hollinsworth right behind. He stopped long enough to knock some street dust off his shoes, then made his way deeper into Ellis Square with all deliberation, feeling Tullidge's eyes boring into his back from the still open door. Silent, he walked through the square until he found a secluded spot by a hedge, where he promptly threw up.

From somewhere, Mr Hollinsworth must have found a damp cloth. He wiped Jem's face.

'Well done, Captain. I am impressed.'

'You realise I'm going to die tomorrow morning and Teddy will be in that man's hands after Christmas day,' he said, sucking on a clean corner of the cloth.

'Pish-posh, ye of little faith,' Hollinsworth said. 'I'm not named Osgood N. Hollinsworth for nothing.'

'What, pray tell, is *that* supposed to mean?' Jem asked, as equal measures of terror and exasperation seemed to roll down his back in waves like sweat.

'In good time, lad, in good time,' Hollinsworth said, and patted Jem's shoulder. 'I am certain I can talk my dentist friend Jephthah Morton into being your surgeon. His life has been a little slow, of late.'

'You're enjoying this,' Jem accused.

'Guilty as charged,' the printer said, looking not even slightly repentant. 'I will arrange for a small sailing vessel to take us to Tybee.' He ticked off his fingers. 'I'll need a table for the pistols, the dentist, and perhaps another observer.'

'An undertaker?' Jem asked.

'Oh, mercy no!' Hollinsworth said with a laugh. 'We need an impartial fellow to examine the pistols, once they're loaded. Go on now. Have a good dinner. I'll make all the arrangements. Aren't you going to meet Miss Winnings at Christ Church tonight for a little cuddle in one of the pews?'

How did Hollinsworth know *that*? 'Aye, that is my plan,' he admitted. 'Then I suppose I am to go back to the Arundel, pay my bill, get a good night's rest, and prepare to die at eight of the clock.'

'Have faith, laddie,' Hollinsworth said, his eyes calm.

Why do I keep hearing that? Jem asked himself. *I must be going mad.*

'You're quite sane,' the printer replied, as if he could read Jem's thoughts. 'Love does that to people, I hear. Toodle-loo until tomorrow.'

'Seven o'clock dockside?'

'You took the words from my mouth, laddie,' Hollinsworth replied, all good cheer. 'Get a good night's sleep.'

You, sir, are certifiable, he thought, but smiled at the old fool anyway.

'Takes one to know one,' Hollinsworth teased.

They parted in the square, Hollinsworth waddling off and humming, and Jem sitting on a bench, grateful none of his brother captains could see him now, with bats in his belfry, ready to duel to the death for a woman.

'I was a reasonable man once,' he said in amazement.

A cat slinking through the underbrush hissed at

him. 'Let's see you do any better,' he said, as the stray arched his back, darted sideways in that way of felines, and disappeared. 'At least it isn't raining yet.'

He sighed as large drops began to pelt down, coming faster and faster until he was drenched.

Really, Sir, he thought. *Can this get any worse?*

It was a good question. He did something he had never done before when addressing *Sir*, his silent partner through most of his life, even though he had only recently acknowledged it. He listened. He watched.

He didn't hear any words, but he wasn't expecting words. He waited in silence and then appreciation as the rain stopped, and a rainbow arched through the sky. It stretched from a great height right down to the Savannah River.

In all his years at sea, the only thing remotely resembling this splendour had been Northern Lights, seen in breathtaking majesty in the far north latitudes. Rapt, he had watched glowing pulses of light, and on another occasion, the somehow sinister ripple of a green curtain. And there was the sprightly dance of St Elmo's Fire from mast to yardarm to the very sheets themselves. Even the most hardened sailor had stared in wonder.

The welcome sight of the Southern Cross in the Antipodes made him pause and reflect, but nothing made his heart as happy as this lovely display. He watched in delight as a smaller rainbow appeared below the larger one, almost as if seeking protection.

He swallowed and thought of Theodora Winnings, who needed him as she had never needed anyone. He was a captain, used to the awful burden of stewardship over every soul in each ship he commanded. He took his duty as a matter of course. He knew he was looking at duty right now, the sort of duty requiring courage above and beyond the simple working of a ship, or even sailing into battle.

This duty was for him alone, special, intimate and feeling less onerous by the second. He was Theodora Winnings' protector. Years may have passed, but his letter offering protection remained valid and in force, even though he had not known when he wrote his letter just what that meant. Did any man?

'I don't know how I am going to win, *Sir*,' he spoke to the sky. He knew he wasn't whining; he really *didn't* know.

Or did he? He watched the rainbows hang there and gradually fade as the light shifted and dusk approached. Hadn't every one and every thing since Mrs Fillion's dining room been telling him? This was faithful service he would give gladly, no matter the outcome, because it was the honourable thing to do. All it required was faith.

Faith. He waited for it to seem corny and foolish and the stuff of boring sermons, but it did not. *Fair enough, Sir*, he thought. *Fair enough.*

Chapter Eleven

Eating was out of the question. Even after his peculiar epiphany, Jem knew nothing would stay down. He spent a few quiet moments at the front desk, paying for his stay, and assuring the clerk he would be gone by morning.

He tried to breathe deep, slow his heartbeat and remind himself what he had just learned in Ellis Square. Why did such a prosaic phrase as 'gone by morning' set his heart racing, and his pulse pounding?

When the clerk had expressed polite dismay at his leaving, and wished him all the best in his journey, why had Jem's thoughts turned to that journey from which no traveller returns? 'Good Lord, the man is only making conversation' vied with 'Repent and prepare to meet your Maker.'

He had faith, but he knew there was something he still lacked, the one ingredient that would get him through this ordeal, however it turned out. No matter; he had enough faith to buoy him into believing he would know what it was before the moment he aimed and fired tomorrow.

Maybe it was also enough to know the identity of that Sir he had been addressing for years, perhaps forgot, and then been so forcefully reminded in Charleston. He relaxed in the chair, smiling to remember sunny days in the South Pacific under full sail, feeling the very pulse of his ship and remembering to thank his silent partner.

'I trust I didn't make a fool of myself too many times, Sir,' he said out loud as he watched the winter sun sink in the west. 'Thank you again for keeping the heart in me when we sailed into battle, Sir. Thank you for the rainbows. I'll do my best tomorrow. Or should I say 'Thank Thee'?'

He closed his eyes and plopped his cares in someone else's generous lap, knowing he had done it many times, but without this new-found awareness. *Call me a late bloomer, Sir*, he thought, satisfied to nap. *I should have known it was Thee all along.*

His natural pragmatism resurfaced. Quite possibly his great good friend the Lord Almighty was far too busy with day-to-day events to concern himself exclusively with one of his sons. It may even have been abominably prideful of him to think Sir was that interested in one puny individual. Besides, Jem knew this was a busy season. Possibly Sir had helpers.

As he lay there half-awake, mostly dozing, he searched his brain to recall if there was a guardian angel for sailors. Whoever he was, Jem was fairly certain that personage or spirit—call him what you will—had been his steady companion through the years. All he could think of right now was St Nicholas, since this was the saint's season of merrymaking and good tidings of great joy. It was enough; he slept.

Jem woke in time to wash his face, comb his hair, put on a new neckcloth and walked to Christ Church, where the choir was straggling in. He singled out the choir master and asked for a moment of his time. Sitting in a pew with him, he told the master he was leaving in the morning for Baltimore.

'Mr Grey, it will be Christmas Eve. You couldn't stay another day or two?' the master asked.

'Times and tides, sir,' Jem said, and the man nodded. Anyone who lived on a waterfront knew what that meant.

'Would you at least sing with us this one last time?' he asked.

There it was again—*one last time*, spoken casually, but words that had weight and heft to them for James Grey, soon-to-be duellist who had courage to spare now, but little skill to fight.

'Alas, no. I will be listening from a back pew, however,' he said, and felt his face grow warm. 'There's a young lady… She's a good friend I knew in another place.'

'Would we know her?' the choirmaster asked. Why did Southerners have to be so politely interested?

'Unlikely,' he said, and quickly changed the subject, because the rector of Christ Church was approaching. 'Excuse me, sir, but I have a question for this good man.'

More pleasantries, and then the question: 'Father, is there a saint or guardian angel for mariners?' Jem asked.

The rector permitted himself a laugh in the church, maybe because Christmas was nearly upon them and he was a tolerant man. 'Mr Grey, I've learned enough about you to know you are a man of the sea, and quite possibly not too observant as a Christian?'

'That might be changing,' Jem said. No need for even a rector to know just how dependent Captain Grey was on his omnipresent Sir, and whatever guardian angel helped out, too. He knew he could never explain the significance of the two rainbows to anyone but Teddy.

Another realisation hit him—was *he* the smaller rainbow, under the protection of a greater one? *Humility*, he thought, relieved, as the last puzzle fell into place. *I can be humble, no matter my circumstances.*

'Mr Grey?'

'Pardon me. I was…uh… I was wool-gathering.'

'To answer your question, it's St Nicholas, the same as blesses our hearts at this season,' the rector said. 'I believe he is also called the wonder-worker, the saint who helps those in trouble. Which would be sailors, you would agree.'

'I would, sir. Wonder-worker. I like that.' Nodding to both men, he walked to the back of the church to wait for Teddy Winnings. *Wonder-worker is it, St Nicholas?* he asked silently. *Work some wonder for me.*

He didn't wait long. Teddy quietly lifted the latch on the gate-like door to the pew and sat down beside him. His heart turned over when she sighed as though she had been holding her breath, or maybe because she suddenly felt safe.

Gone was the slave's bandanna; she wore a bonnet on her curly hair. Her dress was dark blue muslin, worn with a shawl of some Scottish plaid. She wore shoes. She was the loveliest woman he had even seen. He wanted to tell her that, but his natural reticence stopped his tongue, at least until he decided that *Sir* and St Nicholas expected a bit more.

'Teddy, you are lovely,' he whispered. 'I like the bonnet.'

She leaned closer and he breathed in the faintest lavender. 'I was coming here bareheaded, and who should appear but Mr Hollinsworth with this very bonnet. He wished me Happy Christmas and insisted I keep it.'

He reminded himself to laugh quietly; the choirmaster had his hands raised for a downbeat. 'He amazes me.'

She looked ahead at the choir, smiling.

'I hope you didn't get in too much trouble today,' he whispered. 'You were gone so long.' He sighed. 'You said Mrs Winnings keeps that hairbrush handy.'

'No trouble at all,' she whispered back, moving closer because the choir had started to sing. He didn't mind. Her breath was soft on his ear. 'So strange. It was as though I had been gone mere minutes, and not hours. She never missed me.'

'A wonder,' he said.

He took her hand and kissed it, then set her hand on his leg, where she patted him. There was so much he wanted to tell her, and he knew time was his enemy. 'Teddy, like most of the captains, I complained about the Peace of Amiens. Mark you, it will end soon enough and we will be at war again with France. No one likes to be cast ashore on half pay, although most of us post captains have amassed enough prize money to not feel quite the pain that a young lieutenant feels.'

'As you were once,' she said. 'My goodness, I fell in love with a pasty-faced, trembling lieutenant with nothing to recommend him, didn't I?'

'And I fell in love with a beautiful lady who was kind enough to tend me.'

'So you thought,' she teased. 'I had no choice.' Her expression changed to kindness itself. 'And then I couldn't leave. Didn't want to.'

'I am grateful for that Treaty now,' he told her, pausing for a few minutes while the choirmaster gave instructions, then nodded to the pianist to continue. 'It gave me a chance to leave the country, spend seven weeks on a sailing vessel, and think.'

'What did you learn?' she asked.

'That in all those years, I have never been out of love with you.' He turned slightly and took both her hands in his. 'If I survive tomorrow, marry me.'

She flinched at his words and he saw tears gather in her eyes. He watched her master them, as she had probably mastered tears all her life. A slave hadn't the luxury of emotion.

'I accepted your proposal eleven years ago,' she reminded him. 'Nothing's changed.' She took a deep breath and another. 'You will survive.'

'But if I don't...' He reached in his pocket for a ticket and handed it to her. 'Don't come to the island with me tomorrow, Teddy. Gather all your possessions, take this and get on the *Molly Bright*, bound for Baltimore. Wear what you are wearing now, and maybe a cloak, if you have one. It's a Baltimore freighter. They won't know your connections here

in Savannah. I visited the wharf and the captain told
me you should be aboard the *Molly* by eight o'clock.'

'I would rather come with you to Tybee Island,'
she told him.

'You might not like what you see, and there would
be no escaping after that,' he said bluntly. He took
a packet from his coat. 'Here is seven hundred and
fifty dollars.'

She put her hand to her mouth and her eyes grew
wide. 'No, no.'

'Seven hundred and fifty dollars,' he repeated,
showing her two letters in the packet. 'This one
is from Carter and Brustein in Plymouth, where
I bank. It is permission to transfer all funds from
there to a bank or counting house of my choosing
in the United States. In this letter, I've notarized everything over to Theodora Winnings. I want you to
go to Massachusetts and settle there. Do what you
wish once you are there, and remember me. Take
it. You must.'

Lips tight together, her eyebrows drawn down into
a deep frown, she took the packet. She closed her
eyes and bowed her forehead against the pew in
front of them. Without a word, she dropped to her
knees onto the prayer bench.

He knelt beside her, no thought in his head except
the word *Sir* over and over. It calmed him.

A hush fell over the church as the choir finished

'Come, Thou Long-Expected Jesus.' The notes hung on the incense-fragrant air. The peace of the season settled on James Grey, reminding him of a warm blanket placed around his body by a surgeon after the battle of Camperdown, once the man stitched a sabre wound on Jem's thigh. He felt the same drowsy somnolence, and thought he might even sleep to-night.

He walked Teddy Winnings home through magnolia-scented air. There was enough breeze to set the Spanish moss swaying in the oak trees near Green Square. They had started with his arm properly crooked out and hers threaded through it. As they approached the little house and Teddy slowed down, his arm went around her waist, and hers around his.

He kissed her at the back door of the darkened house, holding her close and kissing her several times more. With an ache, he noted how well they fit together. He knew she would not object if he came inside with her and stayed the night in her bed. She was tugging gently on his hand right now, the door open. He also knew what folly that could become, if he got her with child as his last act in mortality.

He told her that as she tugged on him. She nodded and released his hand, but not before kissing it, placing it against her face, and kissing his palm.

'I hope to see you on the deck of the *Molly Bright*, when I climb up the chains from a little boat. After I'm done with Tybee Island,' he said as he backed away.

'You'll see me, dearest sir,' she said, went inside and quietly closed the door.

Chapter Twelve

He did sleep, waking to a quiet knock he had requested from the desk clerk. He lay there a moment, thinking how inexorably time was going to rule for the next few hours. The emotion reminded him of sailing into battle, knowing nothing was going to change the forward movement. Once engaged, whatever puny skills he possessed, or those of his crew, would be put to the test until the issue was decided.

He knew how paltry his talent for this contest, when it came to firearms. He had never been a good shot, choosing wisely to let his Marines aboard his frigates exhibit their marksmanship from the yardarms and ratlines while he stayed out of their way. Too bad he could not post sharpshooters in the trees at Tullidge's plantation.

He washed and dressed with care, not wishing whoever had the task of embalming him to look askance at soiled smallclothes or an untidy neckcloth. He frowned at his nearly full bottle of bay rum, then wondered if he should dump it over his head. It seemed a shame to waste such good fragrance. Perhaps Osgood N. Hollinsworth would use it.

Dressed and with his duffel packed, he shouldered it and went across the street, stopping to eat a bowl of hominy grits, for which he had discovered a fondness during his Southern sojourn. He ate a few bites of shirred eggs, just to placate the cook one last time. The woman was a bit of a martinet.

One block, and he stood on the dock, spending a moment to admire the early-morning bustle, something he was long familiar with, and which never failed to lift his heart, even this last morning in Savannah, possibly his last morning on the planet. Another rainbow would have been reassuring, but the sky was bright with dawn.

Hollinsworth had said there would be a sailboat tied up and ready at the wharf, and he was right. Jem felt his heart sink to see Teddy already seated amidships, a small satchel in her arms.

'You are supposed to take the *Molly Bright*,' he commented as he sat beside her.

'And leave you alone?' she asked. 'I could no more do that than fly.' She twined her arm through his, content to rest her head on his shoulder.

'When we get to Tybee Island, at least stay in the boat,' he insisted, well aware he had lost this round to a determined woman, and thank goodness for that. Argue with himself all he wanted, he knew he did not care to face this dreadful ordeal alone. 'Stay in the boat at Tybee! That way, Mr Hollinsworth can still see you to the *Molly* in the channel…after.'

'Perhaps,' she replied.

He heard no compliance. Obviously he needed to take another tack. 'See here, Teddy, if by some mysterious, highly unlikely miracle I survive this ordeal, am I to gather that you will oppose me whenever it feels right and just to you?' A potential husband ought to know these things, after all.

'You could gather that,' she agreed. 'I have opinions.' She folded her hands in her lap and stared straight ahead. The sides of the bonnet hide her profile, but Jem hoped she was smiling.

In short order Jephthah Morton joined them, carrying his black leather bag and wearing a shiny black suit with a funereal cast to it. Next came Mr Hollinsworth lugging a wooden folding table, which he stowed aboard. He held out his hand to steady a gentleman unknown to James.

He was dressed in black, as Jem suddenly realised they all were, with the exception of Teddy in her blue muslin and brown cloak. Jem swallowed, wishing he could scare up some saliva. Nothing.

'James, may I present Constantine Larkin, Esquire, of Charleston. Max, this is Captain James Grey, late of the Royal Navy,' Hollinsworth said.

Jem couldn't help wincing at 'late.'

'Not late yet, sir,' he said, as he bowed but did not rise in the bobbing craft. Or perhaps he was precisely that. A glance at the lovely woman seated so calmly beside him told him that if he survived, he was staying in the United States, whether the nation wanted him or not. Maybe he *was* late of the Royal Navy.

'Do the honours, Jem?' Hollinsworth asked and indicated the tiller.

Jem moved aft and took the tiller. A few unnecessary words to the deckhand, who knew his business, sent them into the river and quickly past the *Molly Bright*, with its crew aboard and making ready to begin her voyage up the coast, then into Chesapeake Bay to Baltimore.

'You were supposed to be aboard the *Molly* by now, Teddy,' he reminded his dearest darling, who had cautiously moved back to sit closer to him.

'I had other ideas, Captain Grey,' she said.

'Am I to gather further that if I survive, you will call me Captain Grey when you are perhaps slightly irritated with me?' he asked, enjoying himself as he not thought possible, this close to death. He gave all the credit to his patron saint.

'You could gather that, too,' she said, then made no more comment as she turned her attention toward the receding shore.

He wasn't sure which of the barrier islands was Tybee, but the deckhand kept him on target. By the time they docked at what appeared to be a little-used wharf, fog had begun to roll in from the nearby ocean.

The hand leaped from the boat and caught the line that Mr Hollinsworth threw with surprising skill. Another line aft secured the boat. The printer helped Teddy from the sailboat.

'I want her to stay in the boat,' Jem said. 'Mr Hollinsworth, I want you and your crew to get her to the *Molly* when this is done.'

Why did he feel like no one was listening to him? Perhaps because no one was. 'Please, Teddy,' he tried again. 'You don't want to see this.'

'I'll stay out of sight.' She made no objection when he put his arm around her and pulled her close to his side. 'This fog...'

Mr Hollinsworth seemed to know right where to go. He led out with Mr Larkin from Charleston, followed by the deckhand with the table. Looking like a black-coated heron, the dentist brought up the rear as he stalked along on thin legs.

'This is a strange assembly,' Jem said. 'Pray for me, Teddy.'

'What have I been doing for eleven years?' she asked. 'I'll pray more. Jem, I love you. If things...' She stopped and took several deep breaths. 'I'll follow your instructions to the letter.'

'That's all I ask, dear heart.' He kissed her cheek and pointed her toward a smallish boulder by a tree.

'There's a good place to wait. I don't want Tullidge to spot you.'

She shivered. 'I don't, either. Good luck, Jem. Go with God.'

She didn't make their farewell hard, kissing his cheek and hurrying toward the boulder, where she was soon nearly invisible in the enveloping fog. He followed the muffled sound of two men laughing, and wondered what on earth Mr Hollinsworth and Mr Larkin found amusing about this situation.

He squinted, and soon noticed other figures. Here it came again, that feeling of time moving too fast now, every moment bringing him closer to standing and firing, all for the honour of a woman he adored, and who his enemy saw as chattel to be used and tossed.

I am a long way from England, he thought. *Maybe I always was.*

William Tullidge stood beside a younger man who looked much like him, possibly his son.

'I thought perhaps you had shown the white feather,' was Tullidge's greeting.

'Not I, sir,' Jem said. 'And this is…?'

'My son, Geoffrey, serving as my second,' Tullidge said. 'I've already told him that when I tire of Theodora, I will hand her down to him. He'll be tired of his wife by then.'

Only by supreme effort did Jem tamp down a howl of rage. His eyes bored into Tullidge's smiling, self-satisfied, confident face but he kept his counsel, acutely aware that the slave owner sought to unbalance him even further.

Nice try, you bastard, he thought. *I have fought sea battles that would cause you to make water.*

The roaring in his ears stopped. 'Sir,' was all he said. Tullidge looked his way, but Jem was not addressing him. Mr Hollinsworth came closer to touch his arm. 'Good choice, laddie.'

'Mr Hollinsworth, who *are* you?' he asked.

'A simple printer, and not a very good one,' he replied with a shrug. 'Don't worry about that now.'

Mr Larkin cleared his throat. He stood behind the table that held a highly polished wooden box with brass corners. He indicated the box.

'Mr Tullidge, these are your pistols?'

'They are, and lovely ones, I might add.'

Mr Larkin said nothing to that, but merely stared at the slaver, which made Tullidge shift his feet and mutter something. Mr Larkin held up his hand.

'My old friend Mr Hollinsworth summoned me from Charleston, since I know the rules of Code Duello, and he does not. Sir, you say you loaded these pistols while you waited for us to arrive? You say this on your word as a gentleman, and your honour that all is proper?'

'I do.'

Mr Larkin turned to Jem. 'Have you any objections?'

Jem had many but what could he say? 'None, sir,' he said, pleased at how firm his voice sounded, even as his insides writhed. 'He says he is an honourable man.'

'Very well then, let us be about our business this morning,' Mr Larkin said. He looked at both of them. 'Back to back, if you please. Ah, yes.'

'I have never stood this close to a reeking, cursed captain in the Royal Navy,' Tullidge murmured.

'How odd of you to say that,' Jem whispered back. 'I bathed and doused myself in bay rum this morning, just for you.'

Hollinsworth chuckled, then coughed and look away. Mr Larkin glowered at them both. 'Gentlemen! Kindly pace off fifteen steps, then turn, but do not raise your pistols.'

Sir, keep me brave, Jem thought as he walked away from Tullidge. *It's for Teddy.*

He stopped and turned, then squinted. Good Lord, the fog was thicker.

'This will never do,' Mr Larkin said. 'Take five steps closer, if you will.'

Five steps brought them in sight of each other, as the teasing fog made them visible and dangerously close, then barely visible once more.

'Could you not postpone this duel until later in the day, when the fog burns off?' Mr Larkin asked.

'No, sir.'

'No! I have business in town today.'

'Very well, you idiots. Heed me. You may raise your pistols. I will ask each of you if you are ready to fire. You will reply, but you will not fire until I give the word. Do you understand?'

They did.

'Raise your pistols.'

Jem did as commanded, gratified to see his aim was steady.

Teddy, you will be my last and final thought, he told himself. *Sorry, Sir, but that is the way I feel. Wish I had time to gather more faith.*

He waited. And waited, then jumped in surprise to hear Mr Larkin's voice much closer.

'Gentlemen, put down your pistols.'

Jem lowered his weapon. 'Sir?' he asked Mr Larkin.

'I cannot account for it, but I have the most profound impression that I should look at your pistol. Hand it over, Mr Grey, if you please. Both of you approach the table.'

Mystified, Jem walked toward the table. He glanced at Tullidge and saw a man as puzzled as *he* felt. He watched in curiosity as Mr Larkin pulled back the hammer, then peered closer.

'Stand away, gentlemen,' he said. He pointed the pistol out and down in the direction of the burned-out mansion. He squeezed the trigger. Nothing. He squeezed again. Nothing beyond an audible click.

'Your pistol, Mr Tullidge,' Mr Larkin said, his voice distinctly frosty now.

Wordless, his mouth open in what Jem thought was genuine astonishment, Tullidge complied. Mr Larkin pointed his pistol out and down and fired. The weapon went off with a louder report than Jem expected and he jumped. So did Tullidge.

'Sir, I...'

'Mr Tullidge, for shame,' Mr Larkin said. 'On your honour as a gentleman? What foul business is this?'

'I loaded them both,' Tullidge insisted. 'I am a gentleman.'

His words hung on the foggy air. Jem stared at him, certain he saw nothing in the dueller's eyes but confusion and amazement. *I believe you*, he thought. *I truly do.*

'I declare this duel null and void,' Mr Larkin said. He stepped close to Tullidge until the man backed up. 'Mr Tullidge, do you know who I am?'

'Uh...well...a man from Charleston? I know the n-name Larkin is prominent there.'

'Indeed it is, sir. I own and edit the new *Charleston Post*.'

'He does,' Mr Hollinsworth said, speaking up for the first time. 'I should dislike the man, because I know his influential paper quite overshadowed my little Savannah *Times and Tides*. I wanted him here because I know he is a fair man. If you cannot trust a journalist, who can you trust?' He clucked his tongue. 'Mr Tullidge, you disappoint me.'

'But...'

Jem looked from one angry face to the other. Mr Larkin seemed to be just getting warmed up. 'I write a column, sir. *You* will be my subject next week,' Mr Larkin snapped.

'Please no. There is some mistake,' Tullidge said. 'I loaded both of those weapons, upon my honour.'

'Honour? Honour?' Mr Larkin glared at him. 'I can see the headline now—"No honour in Savannah."' He laughed, and the sound held no amusement. 'Just as we suspected in Charleston.'

Silence ruled. Jem looked on Mr Tullidge's face, all colour drained away.

Mr Hollinsworth spoke, his words more conciliatory this time. 'This is harsh indeed, Mr Larkin. You could ruin him.'

'I can and I will, because he is no gentleman,' Mr Larkin said.

'Please no, sir!' Tullidge begged again. He went down on one knee and rested his forehead on that knee.

Jem watched Mr Hollinsworth, and saw something close to unholy glee in his eyes. *What business is this?* he thought. He glanced at Mr Larkin, saw a similar expression, and waited.

Mr Hollinsworth cleared his throat. 'Mr Larkin, what say you do not print that column, although this poor specimen richly deserves to be driven out of Savannah. I am through printing newspapers here, so I will write nothing. I suggest the following conditions.'

'They had better be good, Mr Hollinsworth,' Mr Larkin snapped. 'I am a hard man to convince.'

'Tullidge here allows Mrs Winnings to keep her home that he won at the turn of a card, and gives her five hundred dollars besides,' Mr Hollinsworth said.

'And the slave?' Mr Larkin asked.

'She should be freed. Tullidge here has not an iota of good intentions regarding her.'

Jem glanced toward the boulder where he could plainly see Teddy now. She leaned forward as if straining to hear.

'Well, Tullidge?' Mr Larkin asked, then made what looked like a great show of reluctance to Jem. 'I suppose since this is Christmas Eve, we can be merciful. Do you agree to these terms? You allow Mrs Winnings to keep her house, you pay the widow five hundred dollars, and Teddy goes free.'

Tullidge nodded. 'I agree,' he said in a small voice. 'No gentleman here will ever speak of this morning's work? No one will know?'

'Not one of us will say a word,' Mr Larkin assured him. 'Go on now. Take your duelling pistols and chuck them in the river. Only gentlemen duel and you are no gentleman.'

Jem watched as a broken man picked up the box

with the pistols nestled again in their velveteen frame. He sighed when Tullidge's son shook off his father's hand and walked far away from him. *Can anyone repair that?* he thought, surprised to feel pity.

The man from Charleston, the dentist, the editor and the Royal Navy captain stood close together. 'No gentleman will ever mention this again,' Osgood N. Hollinsworth said, his voice crackling with rare authority. 'Is that understood?'

They all agreed. Jem glanced at the deckhand, who had begun to fold up the wooden table, their business done. The man was silently laughing to himself, his face lively, his shoulders shaking. No gentleman would speak of it again, but as sure as Jem was about to grab up Teddy , running toward him now, he knew without a doubt that the deckhand was under no constraint to remain silent.

What's more, he knew the gentlemen in this strange cabal on foggy Tybee Island knew it, too. Before nightfall, the story of William Tullidge's moral lapse and lack of honour in a duel, in a place where such things mattered, would have circulated far beyond River Street. The story would be whispered from dock slaves to house slaves, to genteel ladies in their boudoirs to their honourable husbands. By the time Christmas Day tomorrow was a gentle memory of too much ham and turkey consumed, and too many drinks downed, Tullidge would be ruined anyway. He almost felt sorry for the man. Almost.

Chapter Thirteen

The timing could not have been more impeccable; Jem felt justified to dub it miraculous. The *Molly Bright* swung into the channel in the calm place right before the river met the Atlantic Ocean. Jem assured a terrified Theodora Winnings that she wasn't going to drop into the channel on her way to *Molly*'s deck.

'Look you there, my love,' he said. 'The deckhands have already rigged a bowline slide. Here it comes. Stand up and hold still.'

In tears, she did as he said, raising her arms as he widened the knot and pulled it over her head. When it was snug against her waist and she held the rope in a death grip, he gave the worldwide signal for them to pull. She shrieked, the deckhands chuckled, and Teddy Winnings went up the side in a flash of skirt, petticoats, and handsome legs that he only peeked at, because he was a gentleman.

He turned to Mr Hollinsworth. 'I think I am on

to you,' he said, which brought a smile to the editor, and a modest ducking of his head. 'One question. Who are man from Charleston and the dentist *really*?'

'People who have owed me favours through the centuries,' he said.

'Will I owe you a favour now?' Jem asked. 'Just curious.'

'That's more than one question, laddie. I'll ask one small favour in a few months. Hug me and get aboard that ship. Times and tides are out of my control.'

After he embraced Mr Hollinsworth, Jem followed Teddy to the deck by climbing the chains.

The grinning deckhand in the sailboat sent their luggage topside when the rope came down again. Jem gave him a small salute. 'If you ever want a job in Massachusetts, I have a suspicion that Mr Hollinsworth will know my address.' The slave saluted back.

Teddy had retreated as far from the railing as she could, but Jem stayed there, his mind and heart on Mr Hollinsworth in the craft bobbing below. He didn't know what to say. What he *wanted* to say would have branded him as a crazy man and a crackpot. *Sir?* he asked, then immediately knew the right words.

'Thank you, Mr Hollinsworth,' he shouted down, as the sails billowed and *Molly Bright* picked up speed. 'Satisfy my curiosity, once and for all. I know it is another question, but humour me on Christmas Eve. What does your middle initial stand for?'

'Nicholas, of course, laddie. Fair winds,' the little man shouted back.

No one will ever believe this, Jem thought, his eyes on the man in the boat. A sudden rush of fog obscured the smaller boat from his sight. When it cleared, the boat appeared to be one person lighter. He watched the others, who carried on as though nothing had happened.

Molly Bright was a seagoing freighter and soon left the coastal shipping lane. Jem quickly discovered that his intended wife was no mariner. He loved her anyway, but not right then, as she spent the few days of the voyage sitting on the deck of the cabin they shared, a bucket in her lap.

Baltimore couldn't have come soon enough for Theodora. Pale and hungry, she let him help her to a quayside tavern for a hearty luncheon of dry toast and consommé. She recovered enough to glower at him for polishing off crab cakes, more hominy grits and eggs and bacon, washed down with ale.

He knew she was on the mend from monumental *mal de mer* when she filched a strip of bacon from his plate and asked for her own bowl of grits. Satisfied and not a little relieved, he watched her eat.

He knew how great her courage was when he suggested they spend the night in Baltimore to allow her to recover. She shook her head, even though he could nearly feel her exhaustion. 'No, sir. We will take the next stage to Philadelphia. I will not spend another moment in the South,' she said quietly, but with fervour.

They were married two days later in the City of Brotherly Love. One of their fellow travellers on the stage from Baltimore to Philadelphia was a lawyer well acquainted with the new nation's matrimonial rules. In fact, he walked them to the courthouse, where he located a magistrate and explained the situation, even though it was closing time and everyone was headed home. New Year's Eve was nearly upon them.

The magistrate asked a few gentle questions, which they answered honestly. He didn't hesitate over Teddy's quiet admission of slavery, and Jem's own declaration of his status as a captain in the Royal Navy, but a native-born son of Massachusetts.

He shook his head when both of them offered documents. 'I don't need to see them,' he said. 'Your honour and right intentions are obvious to anyone looking at you both.'

He married them, stamped the document and took the liberty of kissing Theodora Grey's cheek, after a glance at Jem for permission.

His new wife was silent as they walked down the steps and stood on the sidewalk full of lawyers, office workers and passers-by heading for homes and dinner and a quiet evening before the fire. Theodora shivered in her light Georgia cloak. He generously whisked his cape around both of them as they stood to the side of people passing, and stared at their marriage license from the state of Pennsylvania.

For what turned out to be the final time, his jaw ceased aching. 'Theodora Grey,' he whispered in her ear as her shaking finger traced the words. 'You're safe now. You're my wife and under my protection.'

Trust Teddy to know him already. 'And you're safe, too, dearest,' she told him. 'You're home.'

She was too exhausted for any sort of wedding night beyond cuddling close to him in the first bed they shared as husband and wife. By morning, she agreed to bare her shoulders and show him where Mrs Winnings had laid on that hairbrush. By the time he finished kissing each mark, Jem was willing—no, eager to show Teddy Grey that wicked sabre cut on his thigh.

Events moved along swiftly after that. Her tender touch and the serious comment, belied by her laughing eyes, how relieved she was that the sabre hadn't cut any higher made him gather her close, and prove that everything had healed well and he was in no way impaired.

'Perhaps I should mail your surgeon some special something from the United States to express my gratitude,' his wife said a half hour later after matters had taken their logical course and the room had stopped spinning.

"Some special something'?" he teased. 'Teddy, I know you are generally more articulate than that.'

'Give me time,' she replied with some dignity, then ruined it by kissing his whole scar, giggling the entire length and width of it.

If he had spent a more wonderful week in his life, James Grey couldn't remember it. Room service most obligingly kept them fed. The weather cooperated divinely—oh, that word—by rain turning to snow until only idiots would venture out of doors. And the Greys were anything but stupid.

By the end of the week, though, Teddy insisted on leaving the hotel to stand in the lightly falling snow. His heart tender, he watched as she stared like a child at the tiny, individual snowflakes highlighted against her cloak.

'She's from Georgia. Hasn't seen snow before,' he commented to one of the passers-by who smiled at them, and tipped his hat.

One afternoon when they were contemplating each other's bare toes, Jem admitted to some uncertainty about their next move. 'I want to go to Massachusetts—well, you remember the letter I gave you...'

'Oh, my, I forgot,' Teddy said and got out of bed, wrapping the sheet around her that had come loose from its moorings.

He smiled at the sight of her innate modesty, still

covering up when the matter was entirely unnecessary. He rose on one elbow as she picked through her satchel until she found a letter. She handed it to him, and abandoned modesty by dropping the sheet and sitting cross legged beside him.

An hour later, they got around to the letter, crumpled now and underneath her. 'Mr Hollinsworth told me to give it to you when we reached Philadelphia.' She blushed. 'I forgot.'

He laughed, straightened it out, and pulled her close so they could read it together. 'That man,' he said when he finished. 'He gave this to you *when*?'

'I was eating chicken and you had gone out back to the necessary, I think,' she said. 'You know, that first day we met again.'

'That was before anything had happened. Days before the duel.' Why he thought to argue the matter escaped him. Osgood Nicholas Hollinsworth had proved himself capable of anything, as any good wonder-worker might.

'Where's New Bedford?' she asked, pointing to the words.

'It's a seaport due south of Boston,' he told her. 'Frankly, I would have thought he might recommend Nantucket, which is more up and coming, in my opinion,' he said. 'But no, he says we should go to New Bedford.' He thought about both places and had a quiet laugh inside. Teddy would have to cross open water to get to Nantucket Island, and he didn't relish *that* scene. He had been a husband a mere few days, and he already knew where not to venture.

She took the letter from his chest and nudged him over so she could share his pillow. "'There is a man there, name of Benjamin Russell, who is looking for a partner in a shipbuilding enterprise. Tailor-made for you, laddie,'" she read. She returned the letter to his chest. 'We had better start economizing right now, husband, if that money of yours is our future. How much have we spent?'

'You mean the seven hundred and fifty dollars?' he asked. 'Barely fifty.' He started to laugh then, stopping when she gave him a less than genteel poke in his ribs.

'You are up to something, husband,' she accused.

'Not really, wife,' he joked. 'Did you look at that letter from Carter and Brustein?'

Her eyes troubled, Teddy shook her head. 'I couldn't. I didn't want to bring you bad luck in the duel.'

What a tender woman she was. 'You have no idea what I am worth, in navy salvage and prize money.' He whispered the figure in her ear and she gasped.

After she caught her breath, she told him they were getting dressed and she was going to find a modiste for new clothes. 'You can afford me.'

He couldn't have agreed more. By the time they left Philadelphia ten days later, Mrs Grey looked like the stylish wife of a seafaring man about to change careers.

He wrote a letter to Osgood N. Hollinsworth the night before they left Philadelphia in a private chaise, thanking him for everything and assuring him he had made Theodora his bride at the first opportunity. He invited the little round fellow to visit them in New Bedford.

He had no idea where to mail the letter. On one of their admittedly few jaunts about Philadelphia he had asked a priest about St Nicholas. The priest had informed him of St Nicholas's birth in Patara, in Asia Minor. On a whim, he addressed the letter to *Patara, Asia Minor,* and put it just outside their door, next to his shoes to be shined. To his delight, but not his surprise, the letter was gone in the morning.

He wrote another letter to Michael Cameron, the proprietor of the Marlborough Dining Room, where he had taken many a meal during his Savannah visit, and where they had struck up slightly more than a nodding acquaintance. He had some questions.

After a spine-jostling ride over awful winter roads, they arrived in New Bedford in mid-February, both of them resolved never to travel again. Teddy was pale and nauseous, and well-acquainted with the basin in each of the inns where they stopped. By the last night on the road, she suggested with a blush that maybe it wasn't merely travel sickness. He had a silly grin on his face when he folded her in his arms.

Events moved much as Mr Hollinsworth had predicted in his letter. Benjamin Russell, a man about his own age, was easy to locate in the seaport. He was well-known as an innovative builder who needed more capital to fulfil what no one on the docks doubted would be the making of both Russell and New Bedford. A few evenings together while they chatted in Benjamin's study and their wives knitted and got acquainted in the sitting room, marked the beginning of Russell and Grey Shipworks. Both men argued that the other's name should go first. The matter was settled with a coin toss.

Formal papers were drawn up, and the two couples went in search of a suitable house for the Greys. Jem's only stipulation was that it overlook the water. Teddy requested lots of bedchambers. Furniture and rugs followed. Months later, a much-travelled letter arrived from Savannah, Georgia. Her face betraying her worry, Teddy brought the letter to Jem in his new office. She shook her head at the untidiness of blue prints and ship models, and handed it to him.

He kissed her forehead and massaged the frown line between her eyes. 'No fears. We're a long way from Georgia,' he reminded her. 'Have a seat.'

One chair had blueprints and the other a bolt of canvas, so he held out his arms and she sat on his lap.

'My whole family came to see me,' he said, patting her rounded belly. He opened the letter and held it in front of them both. She finished reading before he did, and she gasped.

'You're too fast for me,' he protested, and pointed to the paragraph where Mr Cameron noted that William Tullidge had left town one night, never to be seen again. Rumours circulated that he had moved west to Mississippi, seeking land not played out by cotton yet, but no one knew for certain. His wife and son had remained in Savannah, and they had nothing to say.

He didn't gasp when he read Mr Cameron's conclusion, although it gave him a jolt.

'Teddy, no one's going to believe this,' he said.

'We won't tell anyone,' she replied. 'Do you think our children will believe us?'

'Hard to say. Not if they're as practical and sceptical as you are. Ow!'

She kissed the ear lobe she had tugged on so hard. 'Saints alive, sir,' she whispered. 'See you tonight.'

After she left, he reread the last two paragraphs of the dining room proprietor's letter that was going to go into his office safe immediately.

Mr Grey, I have to wonder about you. No one has been in that print shop since the end of the revolution. The former editor of Savannah Times and Tides was a Loyalist we ran out of town in 1780. Maybe you meant someone else?

*In fact, the city is demolishing the old eyesore
soon, along with that vacant office next door.
Rumour has it there used to be a dentist there,
but no one is certain.*

'St Nicholas, you are a sly one,' Jem said out loud.
He turned back to the letter. '"As for Osgood N. Hollinsworth, no one can recall anyone by that name.
Ah, well, Tullidge is gone and that is good enough.
Yrs. Sincerely…"'
He put the letter in the safe, certain it would be
gone when he returned in the morning. He was right.
The letter might never have existed, which surprised
him not a bit.
What made his heart turn tender and grateful was
a medal left in its place, similar to one of Teddy's
saints medals she kept in the drawer with her lacy
things. He closed his eyes in gratitude and thanked
the Lord Almighty, who had taken the time in a busy
season to help a man searching for a woman long
gone, and a country never forgotten.
Sir.
When he opened his eyes, he saw a small piece of
paper. He read it with a smile.

*We sometimes get the chance to work some won-
der, laddie. What's Christmas for, if not that?
Name your boy Nicholas James. That is my only
stipulation.*

He slipped the scrap of paper in his pocket, along with the St Nicholas medal that would go in Teddy's drawer. He looked out the window where his partner was getting ready to lay down the keel on their first vessel, one built sturdy and solid and destined to travel the world. He had already suggested to Ben they name it the 'St. Nicholas,' that patron of sailors and children, captives, as well as friend of all in need and jovial guardian of Christmas.

'Wonder-worker, too,' he said as he went to the window and watched, his heart light, his mind at rest, his jaw relaxed. He touched the medal in his pocket, but felt no surprise that the paper had disappeared. No matter. Teddy would be happy to know she was going to have a son. She might argue that it should be James Nicholas rather than Nicholas James, but there was time to change her mind. And St Nicholas was right: It *was* a small favour, one gladly accepted.

'Mr Hollinsworth, there should probably be a Nicholas in each generation from here on out,' he said to the window. 'What say you?'

He felt sudden warmth in the pocket with the medal. 'Aye, then? Aye.'

* * * * *

HER CHRISTMAS TEMPTATION

Christine Merrill

To Nicola Caws. Merry Christmas.